Damaged Goods

Upton Sinclair

Damaged Goods

Copyright © 2022 Bibliotech Press
All rights reserved

The present edition is a reproduction of previous publication of this classic work. Minor typographical errors may have been corrected without note; however, for an authentic reading experience the spelling, punctuation, and capitalization have been retained from the original text.

ISBN: 979-8-88830-015-2

CONTENTS

PREFACE iv
PRESS COMMENTS ON THE PLAY v
CHAPTER I 1
CHAPTER II 16
CHAPTER III 35
CHAPTER IV 50
CHAPTER V 73
CHAPTER VI 89

PREFACE

My endeavor has been to tell a simple story, preserving as closely as possible the spirit and feeling of the original. I have tried, as it were, to take the play to pieces, and build a novel out of the same material. I have not felt at liberty to embellish M. Brieux's ideas, and I have used his dialogue word for word wherever possible. Unless I have mis-read the author, his sole purpose in writing LES AVARIES was to place a number of most important facts before the minds of the public, and to drive them home by means of intense emotion. If I have been able to assist him, this bit of literary carpentering will be worth while. I have to thank M. Brieux for his kind permission to make the attempt, and for the cordial spirit which he has manifested.

Upton Sinclair

PRESS COMMENTS ON THE PLAY

DAMAGED GOODS was first presented in America at a Friday matinee on March 14th, 1913, in the Fulton Theater, New York, before members of the Sociological Fund. Immediately it was acclaimed by public press and pulpit as the greatest contribution ever made by the Stage to the cause of humanity. Mr. Richard Bennett, the producer, who had the courage to present the play, with the aid of his co-workers, in the face of most savage criticism from the ignorant, was overwhelmed with requests for a repetition of the performance.

Before deciding whether of not to present DAMAGED GOODS before the general public, it was arranged that the highest officials in the United States should pass judgment upon the manner in which the play teaches its vital lesson. A special guest performance for members of the Cabinet, members of both houses of Congress, members of the United States Supreme Court, representatives of the Diplomatic corps and others prominent in national life was given in Washington, D.C.

Although the performance was given on a Sunday afternoon (April 6, 1913), the National Theater was crowded to the very doors with the most distinguished audience ever assembled in America, including exclusively the foremost men and women of the Capital. The most noted clergymen of Washington were among the spectators.

The result of this remarkable performance was a tremendous endorsement of the play and of the manner in which Mr. Bennett and his co-workers were presenting it.

This reception resulted in the continuance of the New York performances until mid-summer and is responsible for the decision on the part of Mr. Bennett to offer the play in every city in America where citizens feel that the ultimate welfare of the community is dependent upon a higher standard of morality and clearer understanding of the laws of health.

The WASHINGTON POST, commenting on the Washington performance, said:

The play was presented with all the impressiveness of a sermon; with all the vigor and dynamic force of a great drama; with all the earnestness and power of a vital truth.

In many respects the presentation of this dramatization of a great social evil assumed the aspects of a religious service. Dr. Donald C. Macleod, pastor of the First Presbyterian Church, mounted the rostrum usually occupied by the leader of the orchestra, and announced that the nature of the performance, the sacredness of the play, and the character of the audience gave to the play the significance of a tremendous sermon in behalf of mankind, and that as such it was eminently fitting that a divine blessing be invoked. Dr. Earle Wilfley, pastor of the Vermont Avenue Christian Church, asked all persons in the audience to bow their heads in a prayer for the proper reception of the message to be presented from the stage. Dr. MacLeod then read the Bernard Shaw preface to the play, and asked that there be no applause during the performance, a suggestion which was rigidly followed, thus adding greatly to the effectiveness and the seriousness of the dramatic portrayal.

The impression made upon the audience by the remarkable play is reflected in such comments as the following expressions voiced after the performance:

RABBI SIMON, OF THE WASHINGTON HEBREW CONGREGATION—If I could preach from my pulpit a sermon one tenth as powerful, as convincing, as far-reaching, and as helpful as this performance of DAMAGED GOODS must be, I would consider that I had achieved the triumph of my life.

COMMISSIONER CUNO H. RUDOLPH—I was deeply impressed by what I saw, and I think that the drama should be repeated in every city, a matinee one day for father and son and the next day for mother and daughter.

REV. EARLE WILFLEY—I am confirmed in the opinion that we must take up our cudgels in a crusade against the modern problems brought to the fore by DAMAGED GOODS. The report that these diseases are increasing is enough to make us get busy on a campaign against them.

SURGEON GENERAL BLUE—It was a most striking and telling lesson. For years we have been fighting these condition in the navy. It is high time that civilians awakened to the dangers surrounding them and crusaded against them in a proper manner.

MRS. ARCHIBALD HOPKINS—The play was a powerful presentation of a very important question and was handled in a most admirable manner. The drama is a fine entering wedge for this crusade and is bound to do considerable good in conveying information of a very serious nature.

MINISTER PEZET, OF PERU—There can be no doubt but that the performance will have great uplifting power, and accomplish the good for which it was created. Fortunately, we do not have the prudery in South America that you of the north possess, and have open minds to consider these serious questions.

JUSTICE DANIEL THEW WRIGHT—I feel quite sure that DAMAGED GOODS will have considerable effect in educating the people of the nature of the danger that surrounds them.

SENATOR KERN, OF INDIANA—There can be no denial of the fact that it is time to look at the serious problems presented in the play with an open mind.

Brieux has been hailed by Bernard Shaw as "incomparably the greatest writer France has produced since Moliere," and perhaps no writer ever wielded his pen more earnestly in the service of the race. To quote from an article by Edwin E. Slosson in the INDEPENDENT:

Brieux is not one who believes that social evils are to be cured by laws and yet more laws. He believes that most of the trouble is caused by ignorance and urges education, public enlightenment and franker recognition of existing conditions. All this may be needed, but still we may well doubt its effectiveness as a remedy. The drunken Helot argument is not a strong one, and those who lead a vicious life know more about its risks than any teacher or preacher could tell them. Brieux also urges the requirement of health certificates for marriage, such as many clergymen now insist upon and which doubtless will be made compulsory before long in many of our States.

Brieux paints in black colors yet is no fanatic; in fact, he will be criticised by many as being too tolerant of human weakness. The conditions of society and the moral standards of France are so different from those of America that his point of view and his proposals for reform will not meet with general acceptance, but it is encouraging to find a dramatist who realizes the importance of being earnest and who uses his art in defense of virtue instead of its destruction.

Other comments follow, showing the great interest manifested in the play and the belief in the highest seriousness of its purpose:

There is no uncleanness in facts. The uncleanness is in the glamour, in the secret imagination. It is in hints, half-truths, and suggestions the threat to life lies.

This play puts the horrible truth in so living a way, with such clean, artistic force, that the mind is impressed as it could possibly be impressed in no other manner.

Best of all, it is the physician who dominates the action. There is no sentimentalizing. There is no weak and morbid handling of the theme. The doctor appears in his ideal function, as the modern high-priest of truth. Around him writhe the victims of ignorance and the criminals of conventional cruelty. Kind, stern, high-minded, clear-headed, yet human-hearted, he towers over all, as the master.

This is as it should be. The man to say the word to save the world of ignorant wretches, cursed by the clouds and darkness a mistaken modesty has thrown around a life-and-death instinct, is the physician.

The only question is this: Is this play decent? My answer is that it is the decentest play that has been in New York for a year. It is so decent that it is religious.—HEARST'S MAGAZINE.

The play is, above all, a powerful plea for the tearing away of the veil of mystery that has so universally shrouded this subject of the penalty of sexual immorality. It is a plea for light on this hidden danger, that fathers and mothers, young men and young women, may know the terrible price that must be paid, not only by the generation that violates the law, but by the generations to come. It is a serious question just how the education of men and women, especially young men and young women, in the vital matters of sex relationship should be carried on. One thing is sure, however. The worst possible way is the one which has so often been followed in the past—not to carry it on at all but to ignore it.—THE OUTLOOK.

It (DAMAGED GOODS) is, of course, a masterpiece of "thesis drama,"—an argument, dogmatic, insistent, inescapable, cumulative, between science and common sense, on one side, and love, of various types, on the other. It is what Mr. Bernard Shaw has called a "drama of discussion"; it has the splendid movement of the best Shaw plays, unrelieved—and undiluted—by Shavian paradox, wit, and irony. We imagine that many audiences at the Fulton Theater were astonished at the play's showing of sheer strength as acted drama. Possibly it might not interest the general public; probably it would be inadvisable to present it to them. But no thinking person, with the most casual interest in current social evils, could listen to the version of Richard Bennett, Wilton Lackaye, and their associates, without being gripped by the power of Brieux's message.—THE DIAL.

It is a wonder that the world has been so long in getting hold of this play, which is one of France's most valuable contributions to the drama. Its history is interesting. Brieux wrote it over ten years ago. Antoine produced it at his theater and Paris immediately censored it, but soon thought better of it and removed the ban. During the summer of 1910 it was played in Brussels before crowded houses, for then the city was thronged with visitors to the exposition. Finally New York got it last spring and eugenic enthusiasts and doctors everywhere have welcomed it. —THE INDEPENDENT.

A letter to Mr. Bennett from Dr. Hills, Pastor of Plymouth Church, Brooklyn.

23 Monroe Street Bklyn. August 1, 1913.

Mr. Richard Bennett, New York City, N.Y. My Dear Mr. Bennett:

During the past twenty-one years since I entered public life, I have experienced many exciting hours under the influence of reformer, orator and actor, but, in this mood of retrospection, I do not know that I have ever passed through a more thrilling, terrible, and yet hopeful experience than last evening, while I listened to your interpretation of Eugene Brieux' "DAMAGED GOODS."

I have been following your work with ever deepening interest. It is not too much to say that you have changed the thinking of the people of our country as to the social evil. At last, thank God, this conspiracy of silence is ended. No young man who sees "Damaged Goods" will ever be the same again. If I wanted to build around an innocent boy buttresses of fire and granite, and lend him triple armour against temptation and the assaults of evil, I would put him for one evening under your influence. That which the teacher, the preacher and the parent have failed to accomplish it has been given to you to achieve. You have done a work for which your generation owes you an immeasurable debt of gratitude.

I shall be delighted to have you use my Study of Social Diseases and Heredity in connection with your great reform.

With all good wishes, I am, my dear Mr. Bennett, Faithfully yours,

Newell Dwight Hillis

CHAPTER I

It was four o'clock in the morning when George Dupont closed the door and came down the steps to the street. The first faint streaks of dawn were in the sky, and he noticed this with annoyance, because he knew that his hair was in disarray and his whole aspect disorderly; yet he dared not take a cab, because he feared to attract attention at home. When he reached the sidewalk, he glanced about him to make sure that no one had seen him leave the house, then started down the street, his eyes upon the sidewalk before him.

George had the feeling of the morning after. There are few men in this world of abundant sin who will not know what the phrase means. The fumes of the night had evaporated; he was quite sober now, quite free from excitement. He saw what he had done, and it seemed to him something black and disgusting.

Never had a walk seemed longer than the few blocks which he had to traverse to reach his home. He must get there before the maid was up, before the baker's boy called with the rolls; otherwise, what explanation could he give?—he who had always been such a moral man, who had been pointed out by mothers as an example to their sons.

George thought of his own mother, and what she would think if she could know about his night's adventure. He thought again and again, with a pang of anguish, of Henriette. Could it be possible that a man who was engaged, whose marriage contract had actually been signed, who was soon to possess the love of a beautiful and noble girl—that such a man could have been weak enough and base enough to let himself be trapped into such a low action?

He went back over the whole series of events, shuddering at them, trying to realize how they had happened, trying to excuse himself for them. He had not intended such a culmination; he had never meant to do such a thing in his life. He had not thought of any harm when he had accepted the invitation to the supper party with his old companions from the law school. Of course, he had known that several of these chums led "fast" lives—but, then, surely a fellow could go to a friend's rooms for a lark without harm!

He remembered the girl who had sat by his side at the table. She had come with a friend who was a married woman, and so he had assumed that she was all right. George remembered how embarrassed he had been when first he had noticed her glances at him. But then the wine had begun to go to his head—he was one of those unfortunate wretches who cannot drink wine at all. He had offered to take the girl home in a cab, and on the way he had lost his head.

Oh! What a wretched thing it was. He could hardly believe that it was he who had spoken those frenzied words; and yet he must have spoken them, because he remembered them. He remembered that it had taken a long time to persuade her. He had had to promise her a ring like the one her married friend wore. Before they entered her home she had made him take off his shoes, so that the porter might not hear them. This had struck George particularly, because, even flushed with excitement as he was, he had not forgotten the warnings his father had given him as to the dangers of contact with strange women. He had thought to himself, "This girl must be safe. It is probably the first time she has ever done such a thing."

But now George could get but little consolation out of that idea. He was suffering intensely—the emotion described by the poet in the bitter words about "Time's moving finger having writ." His mind, seeking some explanation, some justification, went back to the events before that night. With a sudden pang of yearning, he thought of Lizette. She was a decent girl, and had kept him decent, and he was lonely without her. He had been so afraid of being found out that he had given her up when he became engaged; but now for a while he felt that he would have to break his resolution, and pay his regular Sunday visit to the little flat in the working-class portion of Paris.

It was while George was fitting himself for the same career as his father—that of notary—that he had made the acquaintance of the young working girl. It may not be easy to believe, but Lizette had really been a decent girl. She had a family to take care of, and was in need. There was a grandmother in poor health, a father not much better, and three little brothers; so Lizette did not very long resist George Dupont, and he felt quite virtuous in giving her sufficient money to take care of these unfortunate people. Among people of his class it was considered proper to take such things if one paid for them.

All the family of this working girl were grateful to him. They adored him, and they called him Uncle Raoul (for of course he had not been so foolish as to give them his true name).

Since George was paying for Lizette, he felt he had the right to control her life. He gave her fair warning concerning his attitude. If she deceived him he would leave her immediately. He told this to her relatives also, and so he had them all watching her. She was never trusted out alone. Every Sunday George went to spend the day with his little "family," so that his coming became almost a matter of tradition. He interested her in church affairs—mass and vespers were her regular occasions for excursions. George rented two seats, and the grandmother went with her to the services. The simple people were proud to see their name engraved upon the brass plate of the pew.

The reason for all these precautions was George's terror of disease. He had been warned by his father as to the dangers which young men encounter in their amours. And these lessons had sunk deep into George's heart; he had made up his mind that whatever his friends might do, he, for one, would protect himself.

That did not mean, of course, that he intended to live a virtuous life; such was the custom among young men of his class, not had it probably ever occurred to his father that it was possible for a young man to do such a thing. The French have a phrase, "l'homme moyen sensuel"—the average sensual man. And George was such a man. He had no noble idealisms, no particular reverence for women. The basis of his attitude was a purely selfish one; he wanted to enjoy himself, and at the same time to keep out of trouble.

He did not find any happiness in the renunciation which he imposed upon himself; he had no religious ideas about it. On the contrary, he suffered keenly, and was bitter because he had no share in the amusements of his friends. He stuck to his work and forced himself to keep regular hours, preparing for his law examinations. But all the time he was longing for adventures. And, of course, this could not go on forever, for the motive of fear alone is not sufficient to subdue the sexual urge in a full-blooded young man.

The affair with Lizette might have continued much longer had it not been for the fact that his father died. He died quite suddenly, while George was away on a trip. The son came back to console his broken-hearted mother, and in the two week they spent in the country together the mother broached a plan to him. The last wish of the dying man had been that his son should be fixed in life. In the midst of his intense suffering he had been able to think about the matter, and had named the girl whom he wished George to marry. Naturally, George waited with some interest to learn who this might be. He was surprised when his mother told him that it was his cousin, Henriette Loches.

He could not keep his emotion from revealing itself in his face. "It doesn't please you?" asked his mother, with a tone disappointment.

"Why no, mother," he answered. "It's not that. It just surprises me."

"But why?" asked the mother. "Henriette is a lovely girl and a good girl."

"Yes, I know," said George; "but then she is my cousin, and—" He blushed a little with embarrassment. "I had never thought of her in that way."

Madame Dupont laid her hand upon her son's. "Yes, George," she said tenderly. "I know. You are such a good boy."

Now, of course, George did not feel that he was quite such a good boy; but his mother was a deeply religious woman, who had no idea of the truth about the majority of men. She would never have got over the shock if he had told her about himself, and so he had to pretend to be just what she thought him.

"Tell me," she continued, after a pause, "have you never felt the least bit in love?"

"Why no—I don't think so," George stammered, becoming conscious of a sudden rise of temperature in his cheeks.

"Because," said his mother, "it is really time that you were settled in life. Your father said that we should have seen to it before, and now it is my duty to see to it. It is not good for you to live alone so long."

"But, mother, I have YOU," said George generously.

"Some day the Lord may take me away," was the reply. "I am getting old. And, George, dear—" Here suddenly her voice began to tremble with feeling—"I would like to see my baby grandchildren before I go. You cannot imagine what it would mean to me."

Madame Dupont saw how much this subject distressed her son, so she went on to the more worldly aspects of the matter. Henriette's father was well-to-do, and he would give her a good dowry. She was a charming and accomplished girl. Everybody would consider him most fortunate if the match could be arranged. Also, there was an elderly aunt to whom Madame Dupont had spoken, and who was much taken with the idea. She owned a great deal of property and would surely help the young couple.

George did not see just how he could object to this proposition, even if he had wanted to. What reason could he give for such a course? He could not explain that he already had a family—with stepchildren, so to speak, who adored him. And what could he say to his mother's obsession, to which she came back again and again—her longing to see her grandchildren before she died? Madame Dupont waited only long enough for George to stammer out a few protestations, and then in the next breath to take them back; after which she proceeded to go ahead with the match. The family lawyers conferred together, and the terms of the settlement were worked out and agreed upon. It happened that immediately afterwards George learned of an opportunity to purchase the practice of a notary, who was ready to retire from business in two months' time. Henriette's father consented to advance a portion of her dowry for this purpose.

Thus George was safely started upon the same career as his father, and this was to him a source of satisfaction which he did not attempt to deny, either to himself of to any one else. George was a cautious young man, who came of a frugal and saving stock. He had always been taught that it was his primary duty to make certain of a reasonable amount of comfort. From his earliest days, he had been taught to regard material success as the greatest goal in life, and he would never have dreamed of engaging himself to a girl without money. But when he had the good fortune to meet one who possessed desirable personal qualities in addition to money, he was not in the least barred from appreciating those qualities. They were, so to speak, the sauce which went with the meat, and it seemed to him that in this case the sauce was of the very best.

George—a big fellow of twenty-six, with large, round eyes and a good-natured countenance—was full blooded, well fed, with a hearty laugh which spoke of unimpaired contentment, a soul untroubled in its deeps. He seemed to himself the luckiest fellow in the whole round world; he could not think what he had done to deserve the good fortune of possessing such a girl as Henriette. He was ordinarily of a somewhat sentimental turn—easily influenced by women and sensitive to their charms. Moreover, his relationship with Lizette had softened him. He had learned to love the young working girl, and now Henriette, it seemed, was to reap the benefit of his experience with her.

In fact, he found himself always with memories of Lizette in his relationships with the girl who was to be his wife. When the engagement was announced, and he claimed his first kiss from his bride-to-be, as he placed a ring upon her finger, he remembered the first time he had kissed Lizette, and a double blush suffused his round countenance. When he walked arm and arm with Henriette in the garden he remembered how he had walked just so with the other girl, and he was interested to compare the words of the two. He remembered what a good time had had when he had taken Lizette and her little family for a picnic upon one of the excursion steamers which run down the River Seine. Immediately he decided that he would like to take Henriette on such a picnic, and he persuaded an aunt of Henriette's to go with her as a chaperon. George took his bride-to-be to the same little inn where he had lunch before.

Thus he was always haunted by memories, some of which made him cheerful and some of which made him mildly sad. He soon got used to the idea, and did not find it awkward, except when he had to suppress the impulse to tell Henriette something which Lizette had said, or some funny incident which had happened in the home of the little family. Sometimes he found himself thinking that it was a shame to have to suppress these impulses. There must be something wrong, he thought, with a social system which made it necessary for him to hide a thing which was so obvious and so sensible. Here he was, a man twenty-six years of age; he could not have afforded to marry earlier, nor could he, as he thought, have been expected to lead a continent life. And he had really loved Lizette; she was really a good girl. Yet, if Henriette had got any idea of it, she would have been horrified and indignant—she might even have broken off the engagement.

And then, too, there was Henriette's father, a personage of great dignity and importance. M. Loches was a deputy of the French

Parliament, from a district in the provinces. He was a man of upright life, and a man who made a great deal of that upright life—keeping it on a pedestal where everyone might observe it. It was impossible to imagine M. Loches in an undignified or compromising situation—such as the younger man found himself facing in the matter of Lizette.

The more he thought about it the more nervous and anxious George became. Then it was decided it would be necessary for him to break with the girl, and be "good" until the time of his marriage. Dear little soft-eyed Lizette—he did not dare to face her personally; he could never bear to say good-by, he felt. Instead, he went to the father, who as a man could be expected to understand the situation. George was embarrassed and not a little nervous about it; for although he had never misrepresented his attitude to the family, one could never feel entirely free from the possibility of blackmail in such cases. However, Lizette's father behaved decently, and was duly grateful for the moderate sum of money which George handed him in parting. He promised to break the news gently to Lizette, and George went away with his mind made up that he would never see her again.

This resolution he kept, and he considered himself very virtuous in doing it. But the truth was that he had grown used to intimacy with a woman, and was restless without it. And that, he told himself, was why he yielded to the shameful temptation the night of that fatal supper party.

He paid for the misadventure liberally in remorse. He felt that he had been a wretch, that he had disgraced himself forever, that he had proved himself unworthy of the pure girl he was to marry. So keen was his feeling that it was several days before he could bring himself to see Henriette again; and when he went, it was with a mind filled with a brand-new set of resolutions. It was the last time that he would ever fall into error. He would be a new man from then on. He thanked God that there was no chance of his sin being known, that he might have an opportunity to prove his new determination.

So intense were his feelings that he could not help betraying a part of them to Henriette. They sat in the garden one soft summer evening, with Henriette's mother occupied with her crocheting at a decorous distance. George, in reverent and humble mood, began to drop vague hints that he was really unworthy of his bride-to-be. He said that he had not always been as good as he should have been; he said that her purity and sweetness had awakened in him new ideals; so that he felt his old life had been full of blunders. Henriette, of course, had but the vaguest of ideas as to what the blunders of a tender and generous young man like George might be. So she only loved him the more for his humility, and was flattered to have such a fine effect upon him, to awaken in him such moods of exaltation. When he told her that all men were bad, and that no man was worthy of such a beautiful love, she was quite ravished, and wiped away tears from her eyes.

It would have been a shame to spoil such a heavenly mood by telling the real truth. Instead, George contented himself with telling of the new resolutions he had formed. After all, they were the things which really mattered; for Henriette was going to live with his future, not with his past.

It seemed to George a most wonderful thing, this innocence of a young girl, which enabled her to move through a world of wickedness with unpolluted mind. It was a touching thing; and also, as a prudent young man could not help realizing, a most convenient thing. He realized the importance of preserving it, and thought that if he ever had a daughter, he would protect her as rigidly as Henriette had been protected. He made haste to shy off from the subject of his "badness" and to turn the conversation with what seemed a clever jest.

"If I am going to be so good," he said, "don't forget that you will have to be good also!"

"I will try," said Henriette, who was still serious.

"You will have to try hard," he persisted. "You will find that you have a very jealous husband."

"Will I?" said Henriette, beaming with happiness—for when a woman is very much in love she doesn't in the least object to the man's being jealous.

"Yes, indeed," smiled George. "I'll always be watching you."

"Watching me?" echoed the girl with a surprised look.

And immediately he felt ashamed of himself for his jest. There could be no need to watch Henriette, and it was bad taste even to joke about it at such a time. That was one of the ideas which he had brought with him from his world of evil.

The truth was, however, that George would always be a suspicious husband; nothing could ever change that fact, for there was something in his own conscience which he could not get out, and which would make it impossible for him to be at ease as a married man. It was the memory of something which had happened earlier in his life before he met Lizette. There had been one earlier experience, with the wife of his dearest friend. She had been much younger than her husband, and had betrayed an interest in George, who had yielded to the temptation. For several years the intrigue continued, and George considered it a good solution of a young man's problem. There had been no danger of contamination, for he knew that his friend was a man of pure and rigid morals, a jealous man who watched his wife, and did not permit her to contract those new relations which are always dangerous. As for George, he helped in this worthy work, keeping the woman in terror of some disease. He told her that almost all men were infected, for he hoped by this means to keep her from deceiving him.

I am aware that this may seem a dreadful story. As I do not want anyone to think too ill of George Dupont, I ought, perhaps, to point out that people feel differently about these matters in France. In judging the unfortunate young man, we must judge him by the customs of his own country, and not by ours. In France, they are accustomed to what is called the MARIAGE DE CONVENANCE. The young girl is not permitted to go about and make her own friends and decide which one of them she prefers for her husband; on the contrary, she is strictly guarded, her training often is of a religious nature, and her marriage is a matter of business, to be considered and decided by her parents and those of the young man. Now, whatever we may think right, it is humanly certain that where marriages are made in that way, the need of men and women for sympathy and for passionate interest will often lead to the forming of irregular relationships after marriage. It is not possible to present statistics as to the number of such irregular relationships in Parisian society; but in the books which he read and in the plays which he saw, George found everything to encourage him to think that it was a romantic and delightful thing to keep up a secret intrigue with the wife of his best friend.

It should also, perhaps, be pointed out that we are here telling the truth, and the whole truth, about George Dupont; and that it is not customary to tell this about men, either in real life or in novels. There is a great deal of concealment in the world about matters of sex; and in such matters the truth-telling man is apt to suffer in reputation in comparison with the truth-concealing one.

Nor had George really been altogether callous about the thing. It had happened that his best friend had died in his arms; and this had so affected the guilty pair that they had felt their relationship was no longer possible. She had withdrawn to nurse her grief alone, and George had been so deeply affected that he had avoided affairs and entanglements with women until his meeting with Lizette.

All this was now in the far distant past, but it had made a deeper impression upon George than he perhaps realized, and it was now working in his mind and marring his happiness. Here was a girl who loved him with a noble and unselfish and whole-hearted love—and yet he would never be able to trust her as she deserved, but would always have suspicions lurking in the back of his mind.

He would be unable to have his friends intimate in his home, because of the memory of what he had once done to a friend. It was a subtle kind of punishment. But so it is that Nature often finds ways of punishing us, without our even being aware of it.

That was all for the future, however. At present, George was happy. He put his black sin behind him, feeling that he had obtained absolution by his confession to Henriette. Day by day, as he realized his good fortune, his round face beamed with more and yet more joy.

He went for a little trip to Henriette's home in the country. It was a simple village, and they took walks in the country, and stopped to refresh themselves at a farmhouse occupied by one of M. Loches' tenants. Here was a rosy and buxom peasant woman, with a nursing child in her arms. She was destined a couple of years later to be the foster-mother of Henriette's little girl and to play an important part in her life. But the pair had no idea of that at present. They simply saw a proud and happy mother, and Henriette played with the baby, giving vent to childish delight. Then suddenly she looked up and saw that George was watching her, and as she read his thoughts a beautiful blush suffused her cheeks.

As for George, he turned away and went out under the blue sky in a kind of ecstasy. Life seemed very wonderful to him just then; he had found its supreme happiness, which was love. He was really getting quite mad about Henriette, he told himself. He could hardly believe that the day was coming when he would be able to clasp her in his arms.

But in the blue sky of George's happiness there was one little cloud of storm. As often happens with storm-clouds, it was so small that at first he paid no attention to it at all.

He noted upon his body one day a tiny ulcer. At first he treated it with salve purchased from an apothecary. Then after a week or two, when this had no effect, he began to feel uncomfortable. He remembered suddenly he had heard about the symptoms of an unmentionable, dreadful disease, and a vague terror took possession of him.

For days he tried to put it to one side. The idea was nonsense, it was absurd in connection with a woman so respectable! But the thought would not be put away, and finally he went to a school friend, who was a man of the world, and got him to talk on the subject. Of course, George had to be careful, so that his friend should not suspect that he had any special purpose in mind.

The friend was willing to talk. It was a vile disease, he said; but one was foolish to bother about it, because it was so rare. There were other diseases which fellows got, which nearly every fellow had, and to which none of them paid any attention. But one seldom met anyone who had the red plague that George dreaded.

"And yet," he added, "according to the books, it isn't so uncommon. I suppose the truth is that people hide it. A chap naturally wouldn't tell, when he knew it would damn him for life."

George had a sick sensation inside of him. "Is it as bad as that?" he asked.

"Of course," said the other, "Should you want to have anything to do with a person who had it? Should you be willing to room with him or travel with him? You wouldn't even want to shake hands with him!"

"No, I suppose not," said George, feebly.

"I remember," continued the other, "an old fellow who used to live out in the country near me. He was not so very old, either, but he looked it. He had to be pushed around in a wheel-chair. People said he had locomotor ataxia, but that really meant syphilis. We boys used to poke all kinds of fun at him because one windy day his hat and his wig were blown off together, and we discovered that he was as bald as an egg. We used to make jokes about his automobile, as we called it. It had a little handle in front, instead of a steering-wheel, and a man behind to push, instead of an engine."

"How horrible!" remarked George with genuine feeling.

"I remember the poor devil had a paralysis soon after," continued the friend, quite carelessly. "He could not steer any more, and also he lost his voice. When you met him he would look at you as it he thought he was talking, but all he could say was 'Ga-ga-ga'."

George went away from this conversation in a cold sweat. He told himself over and over again that he was a fool, but still he could not get the hellish idea out of his mind. He found himself brooding over it all day and lying awake at night, haunted by images of himself in a wheel-chair, and without any hair on his head. He realized that the sensible thing would be for him to go to a doctor and make certain about his condition; but he could not bring himself to face the ordeal—he was ashamed to admit to a doctor that he had laid himself open to such a taint.

He began to lose the radiant expression from his round and rosy face. He had less appetite, and his moods of depression became so frequent that he could not hide then even from Henriette. She asked him once or twice if there were not something the matter with him, and he laughed—a forced and hurried laugh—and told her that he had sat up too late the night before, worrying over the matter of his examinations. Oh, what a cruel thing it was that a man who stood in the very gateway of such a garden of delight should be tormented and made miserable by this loathsome idea!

The disturbing symptom still continued, and so at last George purchased a medical book, dealing with the subject of the disease. Then, indeed, he opened up a chamber of horrors; he made up his mind an abiding place of ghastly images. In the book there were pictures of things so awful that he turned white, and trembled like a leaf, and had to close the volume and hide it in the bottom of his trunk. But he could not banish the pictures from his mind. Worst of all, he could not forget the description of the first symptom of the disease, which seemed to correspond exactly with his own. So at last he made up his mind he must ascertain definitely the truth about his condition.

He began to think over plans for seeing a doctor. He had heard somewhere a story about a young fellow who had fallen into the hands of a quack, and been ruined forever. So he decided that he would consult only the best authority.

He got the names of the best-known works on the subject from a bookstore, and found that the author of one of these books was practicing in Paris as a specialist. Two or three days elapsed before he was able to get up the courage to call on this doctor. And oh, the shame and horror of sitting in his waiting-room with the other people, none of whom dared to look each other in the eyes! They must all be afflicted, George thought, and he glanced at them furtively, looking for the various symptoms of which he had read. Or were there, perhaps, some like himself—merely victims of a foolish error, coming to have the hag of dread pulled from off their backs?

And then suddenly, while he was speculating, there stood the doctor, signaling to him. His turn had come!

CHAPTER II

The doctor was a man about forty years of age, robust, with every appearance of a strong character. In the buttonhole of the frock coat he wore was a red rosette, the decoration of some order. Confused and nervous as George was, he got a vague impression of the physician's richly furnished office, with its bronzes, marbles and tapestries.

The doctor signaled to the young man to be seated in the chair before his desk. George complied, and then, as he wiped away the perspiration from his forehead, stammered out a few words, explaining his errand. Of course, he said, it could not be true, but it was a man's duty not to take any chances in such a matter. "I have not been a man of loose life," he added; "I have not taken so many chances as other men."

The doctor cut him short with the brief remark that one chance was all that was necessary. Instead of discussing such questions, he would make an examination. "We do not say positively in these cases until we have made a blood test. That is the one way to avoid the possibility of mistake."

A drop of blood was squeezed out of George's finger on to a little glass plate. The doctor retired to an adjoining room, and the victim sat alone in the office, deriving no enjoyment from the works of art which surrounded him, but feeling like a prisoner who sits in the dock with his life at stake while the jury deliberates.

The doctor returned, calm and impassive, and seated himself in his office-chair.

"Well, doctor?" asked George. He was trembling with terror.

"Well," was the reply, "there is no doubt whatever."

George wiped his forehead. He could not credit the words. "No doubt whatever? In what sense?"

"In the bad sense," said the other.

He began to write a prescription, without seeming to notice how George turned page with terror. "Come," he said, after a silence, "you must have known the truth pretty well."

"No, no, sir!" exclaimed George.

"Well," said the other, "you have syphilis."

George was utterly stunned. "My God!" he exclaimed.

The doctor, having finished his prescription, looked up and observed his condition. "Don't trouble yourself, sir. Out of every seven men you meet upon the street, in society, or at the theater, there is at least one who has been in your condition. One out of seven—fifteen per cent!"

George was staring before him. He spoke low, as if to himself. "I know what I am going to do."

"And I know also," said the doctor, with a smile. "There is your prescription. You are going to take it to the drugstore and have it put up."

George took the prescription, mechanically, but whispered, "No, sir."

"Yes, sir, you are going to do as everybody else does."

"No, because my situation is not that of everybody else. I know what I am going to do."

Said the doctor: "Five times out of ten, in the chair where you are sitting, people talk like that, perfectly sincerely. Each one believes himself more unhappy than all the others; but after thinking it over, and listening to me, they understand that this disease is a companion with whom one can live. Just as in every household, one gets along at the cost of mutual concessions, that's all. Come, sir, I tell you again, there is nothing about it that is not perfectly ordinary, perfectly natural, perfectly common; it is an accident which can happen to any one. It is a great mistake that people speak if this as the 'French Disease,' for there is none which is more universal. Under the picture of this disease, addressing myself to those who follow the oldest profession in the world, I would write the famous phrase: 'Here is your master. It is, it was, or it must be.'"

George was putting the prescription into the outside pocket of his coat, stupidly, as if he did not know what he was doing. "But, sir," he exclaimed, "I should have been spared!"

"Why?" inquired the other. "Because you are a man of position, because you are rich? Look around you, sir. See these works of art in my room. Do you imagine that such things have been presented to me by chimney-sweeps?"

"But, Doctor," cried George, with a moan, "I have never been a libertine. There was never any one, you understand me, never any one could have been more careful in his pleasures. If I were to tell you that in all my life I have only had two mistresses, what would you answer to that?"

"I would answer, that a single one would have been sufficient to bring you to me."

"No, sir!" cried George. "It could not have been either of those women." He went on to tell the doctor about his first mistress, and then about Lizette. Finally he told about Henriette, how much he adored her. He could really use such a word—he loved her most tenderly. She was so good—and he had thought himself so lucky!

As he went on, he could hardly keep from going to pieces. "I had everything," he exclaimed, "everything a man needed! All who knew me envied me. And then I had to let those fellows drag me off to that miserable supper-party! And now here I am! My future is ruined, my whole existence poisoned! What is to become of me? Everybody will avoid me—I shall be a pariah, a leper!"

He paused, and then in sudden wild grief exclaimed, "Come, now! Would it not be better that I should take myself out of the way? At least, I should not suffer any more. You see that there could not be any one more unhappy than myself—not any one, I tell you, sir, not any one!" Completely overcome, he began to weep in his handkerchief.

The doctor got up, and went to him. "You must be a man," he said, "and not cry like a child."

"But sir," cried the young man, with tears running down his cheeks, "if I had led a wild life, if I had passed my time in dissipation with chorus girls, then I could understand it. Then I would say that I had deserved it."

The doctor exclaimed with emphasis, "No, no! You would not say it. However, it is of no matter—go on."

"I tell you that I would say it. I am honest, and I would say that I had deserved it. But no, I have worked, I have been a regular grind. And now, when I think of the shame that is in store for me, the disgusting things, the frightful catastrophes to which I am condemned—"

"What is all this you are telling me?" asked the doctor, laughing.

"Oh, I know, I know!" cried the other, and repeated what his friend had told him about the man in a wheel-chair. "And they used to call me handsome Raoul! That was my name—handsome Raoul!"

"Now, my dear sir," said the doctor, cheerfully, "wipe your eyes one last time, blow your nose, put your handkerchief into your pocket, and hear me dry-eyed."

George obeyed mechanically. "But I give you fair warning," he said, "you are wasting your time."

"I tell you—" began the other.

"I know exactly what you are going to tell me!" cried George.

"Well, in that case, there is nothing more for you to do here—run along."

"Since I am here," said the patient submissively, "I will hear you."

"Very well, then. I tell you that if you have the will and the perseverance, none of the things you fear will happen to you."

"Of course, it is your duty to tell me that."

"I will tell you that there are one hundred thousand like you in Paris, alert, and seemingly well. Come, take what you were just saying—wheel-chairs. One doesn't see so many of them."

"No, that's true," said George.

"And besides," added the doctor, "a good many people who ride in them are not there for the cause you think. There is no more reason why you should be the victim of a catastrophe than any of the one hundred thousand. The disease is serious, nothing more."

"You admit that it is a serious disease?" argued George.

"Yes."

"One of the most serious?"

"Yes, but you have the good fortune—"

"The GOOD fortune?"

"Relatively, if you please. You have the good fortune to be infected with one of the diseases over which we have the most certain control."

"Yes, yes," exclaimed George, "but the remedies are worse than the disease."

"You deceive yourself," replied the other.

"You are trying to make me believe that I can be cured?"

"You can be."

"And that I am not condemned?"

"I swear it to you."

"You are not deceiving yourself, you are not deceiving me? Why, I was told—"

The doctor laughed, contemptuously. "You were told, you were told! I'll wager that you know the laws of the Chinese concerning party-walls."

"Yes, naturally," said George. "But I don't see what they have to do with it."

"Instead of teaching you such things," was the reply, "it would have been a great deal better to have taught you about the nature and cause of diseases of this sort. Then you would have known how to avoid the contagion. Such knowledge should be spread abroad, for it is the most important knowledge in the world. It should be found in every newspaper."

This remark gave George something of a shock, for his father had owned a little paper in the provinces, and he had a sudden vision of the way subscribers would have fallen off, if he had printed even so much as the name of this vile disease.

"And yet," pursued the doctor, "you publish romances about adultery!"

"Yes," said George, "that's what the readers want."

"They don't want the truth about venereal diseases," exclaimed the other. "If they knew the full truth, they would no longer think that adultery was romantic and interesting."

He went on to give his advice as to the means of avoiding such diseases. There was really but one rule. It was: To love but one woman, to take her as a virgin, and to love her so much that she would never deceive you. "Take that from me," added the doctor, "and teach it to your son, when you have one."

George's attention was caught by this last sentence.

"You mean that I shall be able to have children?" he cried.

"Certainly," was the reply.

"Healthy children?"

"I repeat it to you; if you take care of yourself properly for a long time, conscientiously, you have little to fear."

"That's certain?"

"Ninety-nine times out of a hundred."

George felt as if he had suddenly emerged from a dungeon. "Why, then," he exclaimed, "I shall be able to marry!"

"You will be able to marry," was the reply.

"You are not deceiving me? You would not give me that hope, you would not expose me? How soon will I be able to marry?"

"In three or four years," said the doctor.

"What!" cried George in consternation. "In three or four years? Not before?"

"Not before."

"How is that? Am I going to be sick all that time? Why, you told me just now—"

Said the doctor: "The disease will no longer be dangerous to you, yourself—but you will be dangerous to others."

"But," the young man cried, in despair, "I am to be married a month from now."

"That is impossible."

"But I cannot do any differently. The contract is ready! The banns have been published! I have given my word!"

"Well, you are a great one!" the doctor laughed. "Just now you were looking for your revolver! Now you want to be married within the month."

"But, Doctor, it is necessary!"

"But I forbid it."

"As soon as I knew that the disease is not what I imagined, and that I could be cured, naturally I didn't want to commit suicide. And as soon as I make up my mind not to commit suicide, I have to take up my regular life. I have to keep my engagements; I have to get married."

"No," said the doctor.

"Yes, yes!" persisted George, with blind obstinacy. "Why, Doctor, if I didn't marry it would be a disaster. You are talking about something you don't understand. I, for my part—it is not that I am anxious to be married. As I told you, I had almost a second family. Lizette's little brothers adored me. But it is my aunt, an old maid; and, also, my mother is crazy about the idea. If I were to back out now, she would die of chagrin. My aunt would disinherit me, and she is the one who has the family fortune. Then, too, there is my father-in-law, a regular dragoon for his principles—severe, violent. He never makes a joke of serious things, and I tell you it would cost me dear, terribly dear. And, besides, I have given my word."

"You must take back your word."

"You still insist?" exclaimed George, in despair. "But then, suppose that it were possible, how could I take back my signature which I put at the bottom of the deed? I have pledged myself to pay in two months for the attorney's practice I have purchased!"

"Sir," said the doctor, "all these things—"

"You are going to tell me that I was lacking in prudence, that I should never have disposed of my wife's dowry until after the honeymoon!"

"Sir," said the doctor, again, "all these considerations are foreign to me. I am a physician, and nothing but a physician, and I can only tell you this: If you marry before three or four years, you will be a criminal."

George broke out with a wild exclamation. "No sir, you are not merely a physician! You are also a confessor! You are not merely a scientist; and it is not enough for you that you observe me as you would some lifeless thing in your laboratory, and say, 'You have this; science says that; now go along with you.' All my existence depends upon you. It is your duty to listen to me, because when you know everything you will understand me, and you will find some way to cure me within a month."

"But," protested the doctor, "I wear myself out telling you that such means do not exist. I shall not be certain of your cure, as much as any one can be certain, in less than three or four years."

George was almost beside himself. "I tell you you must find some means! Listen to me, sir—if I don't get married I don't get the dowry! And will you tell me how I can pay the notes I have signed?"

"Oh," said the doctor, dryly, "if that is the question, it is very simple—I will give you a plan to get out of the affair. You will go and get acquainted with some rich man; you will do everything you can to gain his confidence; and when you have succeeded, you will plunder him."

George shook his head. "I am not in any mood for joking."

"I am not joking," replied his adviser. "Rob that man, assassinate him even—that would be no worse crime than you would commit in taking a young girl in good health in order to get a portion of her dowry, when at the same time you would have to expose her to the frightful consequences of the disease which you would give her."

"Frightful consequences?" echoed George.

"Consequences of which death would not be the most frightful."

"But, sir, you were saying to me just now—"

"Just now I did not tell you everything. Even reduced, suppressed a little by our remedies, the disease remains mysterious, menacing, and in its sum, sufficiently grave. So it would be an infamy to expose your fiancee in order to avoid an inconvenience, however great that might be."

But George was still not to be convinced. Was it certain that this misfortune would befall Henriette, even with the best attention?

Said the other: "I do not wish to lie to you. No, it is not absolutely certain, it is probable. And there is another truth which I wish to tell you now: our remedies are not infallible. In a certain number of cases—a very small number, scarcely five per cent—they have remained without effect. You might be one of those exceptions, your wife might be one. What then?"

"I will employ a word you used just now, yourself. We should have to expect the worst catastrophes."

George sat in a state of complete despair.

"Tell me what to do, then," he said.

"I can tell you only one thing: don't marry. You have a most serious blemish. It is as if you owed a debt. Perhaps no one will ever come to claim it; on the other hand, perhaps a pitiless creditor will come all at once, presenting a brutal demand for immediate payment.

Come now—you are a business man. Marriage is a contract; to marry without saying anything—that means to enter into a bargain by means of passive dissimulation. That's the term, is it not? It is dishonesty, and it ought to come under the law."

George, being a lawyer, could appreciate the argument, and could think of nothing to say to it.

"What shall I do?" he asked.

The other answered, "Go to your father-in-law and tell him frankly the truth."

"But," cried the young man, wildly, "there will be no question then of three or four years' delay. He will refuse his consent altogether."

"If that is the case," said the doctor, "don't tell him anything."

"But I have to give him a reason, or I don't know what he will do. He is the sort of man to give himself to the worst violence, and again my fiancee would be lost to me. Listen, doctor. From everything I have said to you, you may perhaps think I am a mercenary man. It is true that I want to get along in the world, that is only natural. But Henriette has such qualities; she is so much better than I, that I love her, really, as people love in novels. My greatest grief—it is not to give up the practice I have bought— although, indeed, it would be a bitter blow to me; my greatest grief would be to lose Henriette. If you could only see her, if you only knew her—then you would understand. I have her picture here—"

The young fellow took out his card-case. And offered a photograph to the doctor, who gently refused it. The other blushed with embarrassment.

"I beg your pardon," he said, "I am ridiculous. That happens to me, sometimes. Only, put yourself in my place—I love her so!" His voice broke.

"My dear boy," said the doctor, feelingly, "that is exactly why you ought not to marry her."

"But," he cried, "if I back out without saying anything they will guess the truth, and I shall be dishonored."

"One is not dishonored because one is ill."

"But with such a disease! People are so stupid. I myself, yesterday—I should have laughed at anyone who had got into such a plight; I should have avoided him, I should have despised him!" And suddenly George broke down again. "Oh!" he cried, "if I were the only one to suffer; but she—she is in love with me. I swear it to you! She is so good; and she will be so unhappy!"

The doctor answered, "She would be unhappier later on."

"It will be a scandal!" George exclaimed.

"You will avoid one far greater," the other replied.

Suddenly George set his lips with resolution. He rose from his seat. He took several twenty-franc pieces from his pocket and laid them quietly upon the doctor's desk—paying the fee in cash, so that he would not have to give his name and address. He took up his gloves, his cane and his hat, and rose.

"I will think it over," he said. "I thank you, Doctor. I will come back next week as you have told me. That is—probably I will."

He was about to leave.

The doctor rose, and he spoke in a voice of furious anger. "No," he said, "I shan't see you next week, and you won't even think it over. You came here knowing what you had; you came to ask advice of me, with the intention of paying no heed to it, unless it conformed to your wishes. A superficial honesty has driven you to take that chance in order to satisfy your conscience. You wanted to have somebody upon whom you could put off, bye and bye, the consequences of an act whose culpability you understand! No, don't protest! Many of those who come here think and act as you think, and as you wish to act; but the marriage made against my will has generally been the source of such calamities that now I am always afraid of not having been persuasive enough, and it even seems to me that I am a little to blame for these misfortunes. I should have been able to prevent them; they would not have happened if those who are the authors of them knew what I know and had seen what I have seen. Swear to me, sir, that you are going to break off that marriage!"

George was greatly embarrassed, and unwilling to reply. "I cannot swear to you at all, Doctor; I can only tell you again that I will think it over."

"That WHAT over?"

"What you have told me."

"What I have told you is true! You cannot bring any new objections; and I have answered those which you have presented to me; therefore, your mind ought to be made up."

Groping for a reply, George hesitated. He could not deny that he had made inquiry about these matters before he had come to the doctor. But he said that he was not al all certain that he had this disease. The doctor declared it, and perhaps it was true, but the most learned physicians were sometimes deceived.

He remembered something he had read in one of the medical books. "Dr. Ricord maintains that after a certain period the disease is no longer contagious. He has proven his contentions by examples. Today you produce new examples to show that he is wrong! Now, I want to do what's right, but surely I have the right to think it over. And when I think it over, I realize that all the evils with which you threaten me are only probable evils. In spite of your desire to terrify me, you have been forced to admit that possibly my marriage would not have any troublesome consequence for my wife."

The doctor found difficulty in restraining himself. But he said, "Go on. I will answer you afterwards."

And George blundered ahead in his desperation. "Your remedies are powerful, you tell me; and for the calamities of which you speak to befall me, I would have to be among the rare exceptions—also my wife would have to be among the number of those rare exceptions. If a mathematician were to apply the law of chance to these facts, the result of his operation would show but slight chance of a catastrophe, as compared with the absolute certainty of a series of misfortunes, sufferings, troubles, tears, and perhaps tragic accidents which the breaking of my engagement would cause. So I say that the mathematician—who is, even more than you, a man of science, a man of a more infallible science—the mathematician would conclude that wisdom was not with you doctors, but with me."

"You believe it, sir!" exclaimed the other. "But you deceive yourself." And he continued, driving home his point with a finger which seemed to George to pierce his very soul. "Twenty cases identical with your own have been patiently observed, from the beginning to the end. Nineteen times the woman was infected by her husband; you hear me, sir, nineteen times out of twenty! You believe that the disease is without danger, and you take to yourself the right to expose your wife to what you call the chance of your being one of those exceptions, for whom our remedies are without effect. Very well; it is necessary that you should know the disease which your wife, without being consulted, will run a chance of contracting. Take that book, sir; it is the work of my teacher. Read it yourself. Here, I have marked the passage."

He held out the open book; but George could not lift a hand to take it.

"You do not wish to read it?" the other continued. "Listen to me."

And in a voice trembling with passion, he read: "'I have watched the spectacle of an unfortunate young woman, turned into a veritable monster by means of a syphilitic infection. Her face, or rather let me say what was left of her face, was nothing but a flat surface seamed with scars.'"

George covered his face, exclaiming, "Enough, sir! Have mercy!"

But the other cried, "No, no! I will go to the very end. I have a duty to perform, and I will not be stopped by the sensibility of your nerves."

He went on reading: "'Of the upper lip not a trace was left; the ridge of the upper gums appeared perfectly bare.'" But then at the young man's protests, his resolution failed him. "Come," he said, "I will stop. I am sorry for you—you who accept for another person, for the woman you say you love, the chance of a disease which you cannot even endure to hear described. Now, from whom did that woman get syphilis? It is not I who am speaking, it is the book. 'From a miserable scoundrel who was not afraid to enter into matrimony when he had a secondary eruption.' All that was established later on—'and who, moreover, had thought it best not to let his wife be treated for fear of awakening her suspicions!'"

The doctor closed the book with a bang. "What that man has done, sir, is what you want to do."

George was edging toward the door; he could no longer look the doctor in the eye. "I should deserve all those epithets and still more brutal ones if I should marry, knowing that my marriage would cause such horrors. But that I do not believe. You and your teachers—you are specialists, and consequently you are driven to attribute everything to the disease you make the subject of your studies. A tragic case, an exceptional case, holds a kind of fascination for you; you think it can never be talked about enough."

"I have heard that argument before," said the doctor, with an effort at patience.

"Let me go on, I beg you," pleaded George. "You have told me that out of every seven men there is one syphilitic. You have told me that there are one hundred thousand in Paris, coming and going, alert, and apparently well."

"It is true," said the doctor, "that there are one hundred thousand who are actually at this moment not visibly under the influence of the disease. But many thousands have passed into our hospitals, victims of the most frightful ravages that our poor bodies can support. These—you do not see them, and they do not count for you. But again, if it concerned no one but yourself, you might be able to argue thus. What I declare to you, what I affirm with all the violence of my conviction, is that you have not the right to expose a human creature to such chances—rare, as I know, but terrible, as I know still better. What have you to answer to that?"

"Nothing," stammered George, brought to his knees at last. "You are right about that. I don't know what to think."

"And in forbidding you marriage," continued the doctor, "is it the same as if I forbade it forever? Is it the same as if I told you that you could never be cured? On the contrary, I hold out to you every hope; but I demand of you a delay of three or four years, because it will take me that time to find out if you are among the number of those unfortunate ones whom I pity with all my heart, for whom the disease is without mercy; because during that time you will be dangerous to your wife and to your children. The children I have not yet mentioned to you."

Here the doctor's voice trembled slightly. He spoke with moving eloquence. "Come, sir, you are an honest man; you are too young for such things not to move you; you are not insensible to duty. It is impossible that I shan't be able to find a way to your heart, that I shan't be able to make you obey me. My emotion in speaking to you proves that I appreciate your suffering, that I suffer with you. It is in the name of my sincerity that I implore you. You have admitted it—that you have not the right to expose your wife to such miseries. But it is not only your wife that you strike; you may attack in her your own children. I exclude you for a moment from my thought—you and her. It is in the name of these innocents that I implore you; it is the future, it is the race that I defend. Listen to me, listen to me! Out of the twenty households of which I spoke, only fifteen had children; these fifteen had twenty-eight. Do you know how many out of these twenty-eight survived? Three, sir! Three out of twenty-eight! Syphilis is above everything a murderer of children. Herod reigns in France, and over all the earth, and begins each year his massacre of the innocents; and if it be not blasphemy against the sacredness of life, I say that the most happy are those who have disappeared. Visit our children's hospitals! We know too well the child of syphilitic parents; the type is classical; the doctors can pick it out anywhere. Those little old creatures who have the appearance of having already lived, and who have kept the stigmata of all out infirmities, of all our decay. They are the victims of fathers who have married, being ignorant of what you know—things which I should like to go and cry out in the public places."

The doctor paused, and then in a solemn voice continued: "I have told you all, without exaggeration. Think it over. Consider the pros and cons; sum up the possible misfortunes and the certain miseries. But disregard yourself, and consider that there are in one side of the scales the misfortunes of others, and in the other your own. Take care that you are just."

George was at last overcome. "Very well," he said, "I give way. I won't get married. I will invent some excuse; I will get a delay of six months. More than that, I cannot do."

The doctor exclaimed, "I need three years—I need four years!"

"No, Doctor!" persisted George. "You can cure me in less time than that."

The other answered, "No! No! No!"

32

George caught him by the hand, imploringly. "Yes! Science in all powerful!"

"Science is not God," was the reply. "There are no longer any miracles."

"If only you wanted to do it!" cried the young man, hysterically. "You are a learned man; seek, invent, find something! Try some new plan with me; give me double the dose, ten times the does; make me suffer. I give myself up to you; I will endure everything— I swear it! There ought to be some way to cure me within six months. Listen to me! I tell you I can't answer for myself with that delay. Come; it is in the name of my wife, in the name of my children, that I implore you. Do something for them!"

The doctor had reached the limit of his patience. "Enough, sir!" he cried. "Enough!"

But nothing could stop the wretched man. "On my knees!" he cried. "I put myself on my knees before you! Oh! If only you would do it! I would bless you; I would adore you, as one adores a god! All my gratitude, all my life—half my fortune! For mercy's sake, Doctor, do something; invent something; make some discovery—have pity!"

The doctor answered gravely, "Do you wish me to do more for you than for the others?"

George answered, unblushingly, 'answered, unblushingly, "Yes!" He was beside himself with terror and distress.

The other's reply was delivered in a solemn tone. "Understand, sir, for every one of out patients we do all that we can, whether it be the greatest personage, or the last comer to out hospital clinic. We have no secrets in reserve for those who are more fortunate, or less fortunate than the others, and who are in a hurry to be cured."

George gazed at him for a moment in bewilderment and despair, and then suddenly bowed his head. "Good-by, Doctor," he answered.

"Au revoir, sir," the other corrected—with what proved to be prophetic understanding. For George was destined to see him again—even though he had made up his mind to the contrary!

CHAPTER III

George Dupont had the most important decision of his life to make; but there was never very much doubt what his decision would be. One the one hand was the definite certainty that if he took the doctor's advice, he would wreck his business prospects, and perhaps also lose the woman he loved. On the other hand were vague and uncertain possibilities which it was difficult for him to make real to himself. It was all very well to wait a while to be cured of the dread disease; but to wait three or four years—that was simply preposterous!

He decided to consult another physician. He would find one this time who would not be so particular, who would be willing to take some trouble to cure him quickly. He began to notice the advertisements which were scattered over the pages of the newspapers he read. There were apparently plenty of doctors in Paris who could cure him, who were willing to guarantee to cure him. After much hesitation, he picked out one whose advertisement sounded the most convincing.

The office was located in a cheap quarter. It was a dingy place, not encumbered with works of art, but with a few books covered with dust. The doctor himself was stout and greasy, and he rubbed his hands with anticipation at the sight of so prosperous-looking a patient. But he was evidently a man of experience, for he knew exactly what was the matter with George, almost without the formality of an examination. Yes, he could cure him, quickly, he said. There had recently been great discoveries made—new methods which had not reached the bulk of the profession. He laughed at the idea of three or four years. That was the way with those specialists! When one got forty francs for a consultation, naturally, one was glad to drag out the case. There were tricks in the medical trade, as in all others. A doctor had to live; when he had a big name, he had to live expensively.

The new physician wrote out two prescriptions, and patted George on the shoulder as he went away. There was no need for him to worry; he would surely be well in three months. If he would put off his marriage for six months, he would be doing everything within reason. And meantime, there was no need for him to worry himself—things would come out all right. So George went away, feeling as if a mountain had been lifted from his shoulders.

He went to see Henriette that same evening, to get the matter settled. "Henriette," he said, "I have to tell you something very important—something rather painful. I hope you won't let it disturb you too much."

She was gazing at him in alarm. "What is it?"

"Why," he said, blushing in spite of himself, and regretting that he had begun the matter so precipitately, "for some time I've not been feeling quite well. I've been having a slight cough. Have you noticed it?"

"Why no!" exclaimed Henriette, anxiously.

"Well, today I went to see a doctor, and he says that there is a possibility—you understand it is nothing very serious—but it might be—I might possibly have lung trouble."

"George!" cried the girl in horror.

He put his hand upon hers. "Don't be frightened," he said. "It will be all right, only I have to take care of myself." How very dear of her, he thought—to be so much worried!

"George, you ought to go away to the country!" she cried. "You have been working too hard. I always told you that if you shut yourself up so much—"

"I am going to take care of myself," he said. "I realize that it is necessary. I shall be all right—the doctor assured me there was no doubt of it, so you are not to distress yourself. But meantime, here is the trouble: I don't think it would be right for me to marry until I am perfectly well."

Henriette gave an exclamation of dismay.

"I am sure we should put it off," he went on, "it would be only fair to you."

"But, George!" she protested. "Surely it can't be that serious!"

"We ought to wait," he said. "You ought not to take the chance of being married to a consumptive."

The other protested in consternation. He did not look like a consumptive; she did not believe that he WAS a consumptive. She was willing to take her chances. She loved him, and she was not afraid. But George insisted—he was sure that he ought not to marry for six months.

"Did the doctor advise that?" asked Henriette.

"No," he replied, "but I made up my mind after talking to him that I must do the fair and honorable thing. I beg you to forgive me, and to believe that I know best."

George stood firmly by this position, and so in the end she had to give way. It did not seem quite modest in her to continue persisting.

George volunteered to write a letter to her father; and he hoped this would settle the matter without further discussion. But in this he was disappointed. There had to be a long correspondence with long arguments and protestations from Henriette's father and from his own mother. It seemed such a singular whim. Everybody persisted in diagnosing his symptoms, in questioning him about what the doctor had said, who the doctor was, how he had come to consult him—all of which, of course, was very embarrassing to George, who could not see why they had to make such a fuss. He took to cultivating a consumptive look, as well as he could imagine it; he took to coughing as he went about the house—and it was all he could do to keep from laughing, as he saw the look of dismay on his poor mother's face. After all, however, he told himself that he was not deceiving her, for the disease he had was quite as serious as tuberculosis.

It was very painful and very trying. But there was nothing that could be done about it; the marriage had been put off for six months, and in the meantime he and Henriette had to control their impatience and make the best of their situation. Six months was a long time; but what if it had been three or four years, as the other doctor had demanded? That would have been a veritable sentence of death.

George, as we have seen, was conscientious, and regular and careful in his habits. He took the medicine which the new doctor prescribed for him; and day by day he watched, and to his great relief saw the troublesome symptoms gradually disappearing. He began to take heart, and to look forward to life with his former buoyancy. He had had a bad scare, but now everything was going to be all right.

Three or four months passed, and the doctor told him he was cured. He really was cured, so far as he could see. He was sorry, now, that he had asked for so long a delay from Henriette; but the new date for the wedding had been announced, and it would be awkward to change it again. George told himself that he was being "extra careful," and he was repaid for the inconvenience by the feeling of virtue derived from the delay. He was relieved that he did not have to cough any more, or to invent any more tales of his interviews with the imaginary lung-specialist. Sometimes he had guilty feelings because of all the lying he had had to do; but he told himself that it was for Henriette's sake. She loved him as much as he loved her. She would have suffered needless agonies had she known the truth; she would never have got over it—so it would have been a crime to tell her.

He really loved her devotedly, thoroughly. From the beginning he had thought as much of her mental sufferings as he had of any physical harm that the dread disease might do to him. How could he possibly persuade himself to give her up, when he knew that the separation would break her heart and ruin her whole life? No; obviously, in such a dilemma, it was his duty to use his own best judgment, and get himself cured as quickly as possible. After that he would be true to her, he would take no more chances of a loathsome disease.

The secret he was hiding made him feel humble—made him unusually gentle in his attitude towards the girl. He was a perfect lover, and she was ravished with happiness. She thought that all his sufferings were because of his love for her, and the delay which he had imposed out of his excess of conscientiousness. So she loved him more and more, and never was there a happier bride than Henriette Loches, when at last the great day arrived.

They went to the Riveria for their honeymoon, and then returned to live in the home which had belonged to George's father. The investment in the notary's practice had proven a good one, and so life held out every promise for the young couple. They were divinely happy.

After a while, the bride communicated to her husband the tidings that she was expecting a child. Then it seemed to George that the cup of his earthly bliss was full. His ailment had slipped far into the background of his thoughts, like an evil dream which he had forgotten. He put away the medicines in the bottom of his trunk and dismissed the whole matter from his mind. Henriette was well—a very picture of health, as every one agreed. The doctor had never seen a more promising young mother, he declared, and Madame Dupont, the elder, bloomed with fresh life and joy as she attended her daughter-in-law.

Henriette went for the summer to her father's place in the provinces, which she and George had visited before their marriage.

They drove out one day to the farm where they had stopped. The farmer's wife had a week-old baby, the sight of which made Henriette's heart leap with delight. He was such a very healthy baby that George conceived the idea that this would be the woman to nurse his own child, in case Henriette herself should not be able to do it.

They came back to the city, and there the baby was born. As George paced the floor, waiting for the news, the memory of his evil dreams came back to him. He remembered all the dreadful monstrosities of which he had read—infants that were born of syphilitic parents. His heart stood still when the nurse came into the room to tell him the tidings.

But it was all right; of course it was all right! He had been a fool, he told himself, as he stood in the darkened room and gazed at the wonderful little mite of life which was the fruit of his love. It was a perfect child, the doctor said—a little small, to be sure, but that was a defect which would soon be remedied. George kneeled by the bedside and kissed the hand of his wife, and went out of the room feeling as if he had escaped from a tomb.

All went well, and after a couple of weeks Henriette was about the house again, laughing all day and singing with joy. But the baby did not gain quite as rapidly as the doctor had hoped, and it was decided that the country air would be better for her. So George and his mother paid a visit to the farm in the country, and arranged that the country woman should put her own child to nurse elsewhere and should become the foster-mother of little Gervaise.

George paid a good price for the service, far more than would have been necessary, for the simple country woman was delighted with the idea of taking care of the grandchild of the deputy of her district. George came home and told his wife about this and had a merry time as he pictured the woman boasting about it to the travelers who stopped at her door. "Yes, ma'am, a great piece of luck I've got, ma'am. I've got the daughter of the daughter of our deputy—at your service ma'am. My! But she is as fat as out little calf—and so clever! She understands everything. A great piece of luck for me, ma'am. She's the daughter of the daughter of our deputy!" Henriette was vastly entertained, discovering in her husband a new talent, that of an actor.

As for George's mother, she was hardly to be persuaded from staying in the country with the child. She went twice a week, to make sure that all went well. Henriette and she lived with the child's picture before them; they spent their time sewing on caps and underwear—all covered with laces and frills and pink and blue ribbons. Every day, when George came home from his work, he found some new article completed, and was ravished by the scent of some new kind of sachet powder. What a lucky man he was!

You would think he must have been the happiest man in the whole city of Paris. But George, alas, had to pay the penalty for his early sins. There was, for instance, the deception he had practiced upon his friend, away back in the early days. Now he had friends of his own, and he could not keep these friends from visiting him; and so he was unquiet with the fear that some one of them might play upon him the same vile trick. Even in the midst of his radiant happiness, when he knew that Henriette was hanging upon his every word, trembling with delight when she heard his latchkey in the door—still he could not drive away the horrible thought that perhaps all this might be deception.

There was his friend, Gustave, for example. He had been a friend of Henriette's before her marriage; he had even been in love with her at one time. And now he came sometimes to the house—once or twice when George was away! What did that mean? George wondered. He brooded over it all day, but dared not drop any hint to Henriette. But he took to setting little traps to catch her; for instance, he would call her up on the telephone, disguising his voice. "Hello! Hello! Is that you, Madame Dupont?" And when she answered, "It is I, sir," all unsuspecting, he would inquire, "Is George there?"

"No, sir," she replied. "Who is this speaking?"

He answered, "It is I, Gustave. How are you this morning?" He wanted to see what she would answer. Would she perhaps say, "Very well, Gustave. How are you?"—in a tone which would betray too great intimacy!

But Henriette was a sharp young person. The tone did not sound like Gustave's. She asked in bewilderment, "What?" and then again, "What?"

So, at last, George, afraid that his trick might be suspected, had to burst out laughing, and turn it into a joke. But when he came home and teased his wife about it, the laugh was not all on his side. Henriette had guessed the real meaning of his joke! She did not really mind—she took his jealousy as a sign of love, and was pleased with it. It is not until a third party come upon the scene that jealousy begins to be annoying.

So she had a merry time teasing George. "You are a great fellow! You have no idea how well I understand you—and after only a year of marriage!"

"You know me?" said the husband, curiously. (It is always so fascinating when anybody thinks she know us better than we know ourselves!) "Tell me, what do you think about me?"

"You are restless," said Henriette. "You are suspicious. You pass your time putting flies in your milk, and inventing wise schemes to get them out."

"Oh, you think that, do you?" said George, pleased to be talked about.

"I am not annoyed," she answered. "You have always been that way—and I know that it's because at bottom you are timid and disposed to suffer. And then, too, perhaps you have reasons for not having confidence in a wife's intimate friends—lady-killer that you are!"

George found this rather embarrassing; but he dared not show it, so he laughed gayly. "I don't know what you mean," he said—"upon my word I don't. But it is a trick I would not advise everybody to try."

There were other embarrassing moments, caused by George's having things to conceal. There was, for instance, the matter of the six months' delay in the marriage—about which Henriette would never stop talking. She begrudged the time, because she had got the idea that little Gervaise was six months younger than she otherwise would have been. "That shows your timidity again," she would say. "The idea of your having imagined yourself a consumptive!"

Poor George had to defend himself. "I didn't tell you half the truth, because I was afraid of upsetting you. It seemed I had the beginning of chronic bronchitis. I felt it quite keenly whenever I took a breath, a deep breath—look, like this. Yes—I felt—here and there, on each side of the chest, a heaviness—a difficulty—"

"The idea of taking six months to cure you of a thing like that!" exclaimed Henriette. "And making our baby six months younger than she ought to be!"

"But," laughed George, "that means that we shall have her so much the longer! She will get married six months later!"

"Oh, dear me," responded the other, "let us not talk about such things! I am already worried, thinking she will get married some day."

"For my part," said George, "I see myself mounting with her on my arm the staircase of the Madeleine."

"Why the Madeleine?" exclaimed his wife. "Such a very magnificent church!"

"I don't know—I see her under her white veil, and myself all dressed up, and with an order."

"With an order!" laughed Henriette. "What do you expect to do to win an order?"

"I don't know that—but I see myself with it. Explain it as you will, I see myself with an order. I see it all, exactly as if I were there—the Swiss guard with his white stockings and the halbard, and the little milliner's assistants and the scullion lined up staring."

"It is far off—all that," said Henriette. "I don't like to talk of it. I prefer her as a baby. I want her to grow up—but then I change my mind and think I don't. I know your mother doesn't. Do you know, I don't believe she ever thinks about anything but her little Gervaise."

"I believe you," said the father. "The child can certainly boast of having a grandmother who loves her."

"Also, I adore your mother," declared Henriette. "She makes me forget my misfortune in not having my own mother. She is so good!"

"We are all like that in our family," put in George.

"Really," laughed the wife. "Well, anyhow—the last time that we went down in the country with her—you had gone out, I don't know where you had gone—"

"To see the sixteenth-century chest," suggested the other.

"Oh, yes," laughed Henriette; "your famous chest!" (You must excuse this little family chatter of theirs—they were so much in love with each other!)

"Don't let's talk about that," objected George. "You were saying—?"

"You were not there. The nurse was out at mass, I think—"

"Or at the wine merchant's! Go on, go on."

"Well, I was in the little room, and mother dear thought she was all alone with Gervaise. I was listening; she was talking to the baby—all sorts of nonsense, pretty little words—stupid, if you like, but tender. I wanted to laugh, and at the same time I wanted to weep."

"Perhaps she called her 'my dear little Savior'?"

"Exactly! Did you hear her?"

"No—but that is what she used to call me when I was little."

"It was that day she swore that the little one had recognized her, and laughed!"

"Oh, yes!"

"And then another time, when I went into her room—mother's room—she didn't hear me because the door was open, but I saw her. She was in ecstasy before the little boots which the baby wore at baptism—you know?"

"Yes, yes."

"Listen, then. She had taken them and she was embracing them!"

"And what did you say then?"

"Nothing; I stole out very softly, and I sent across the threshold a great kiss to the dear grandmother!"

Henriette sat for a moment in thought. "It didn't take her very long," she remarked, "today when she got the letter from the nurse. I imagine she caught the eight-fifty-nine train!"

"Any yet," laughed George, "it was really nothing at all."

"Oh no," said his wife. "Yet after all, perhaps she was right—and perhaps I ought to have gone with her."

"How charming you are, my poor Henriette! You believe everything you are told. I, for my part, divined right away the

45

truth. The nurse was simply playing a game on us; she wanted a raise. Will you bet? Come, I'll bet you something. What would you like to bet? You don't want to? Come, I'll bet you a lovely necklace—you know, with a big pearl."

"No," said Henriette, who had suddenly lost her mood of gayety. "I should be too much afraid of winning."

"Stop!" laughed her husband. "Don't you believe I love her as much as you love her—my little duck? Do you know how old she is? I mean her EXACT age?"

Henriette sat knitting her brows, trying to figure.

"Ah!" he exploded. "You see you don't know! She is ninety-one days and eight hours! Ha, ha! Imagine when she will be able to walk all alone. Then we will take her back with us; we must wait at least six months." Then, too late, poor George realized that he had spoken the fatal phrase again.

"If only you hadn't put off our marriage, she would be able to walk now," said Henriette.

He rose suddenly. "Come," he said, "didn't you say you had to dress and pay some calls?"

Henriette laughed, but took the hint.

"Run along, little wife," he said. "I have a lot of work to do in the meantime. You won't be down-stairs before I shall have my nose buried in my papers. Bye-bye."

"Bye-bye," said Henriette. But they paused to exchange a dozen or so kisses before she went away to dress.

Then George lighted a cigarette and stretched himself out in the big armchair. He seemed restless; he seemed to be disturbed about something. Could it be that he had not been so much at ease as he had pretended to be, since the letter had come from the baby's nurse? Madame Dupont had gone by the earliest train that morning. She had promised to telegraph at once—but she had not done so, and now it was late afternoon.

George got up and wandered about. He looked at himself in the glass for a moment; then he went back to the chair and pulled up another to put his geet upon. He puffed away at his cigarette until he was calmer. But then suddenly he heard the rustle of a dress behind him, and glanced about, and started up with an exclamation, "Mother!"

Madame Dupont stood in the doorway. She did not speak. Her veil was thrown back and George noted instantly the look of agitation upon her countenance.

"What's the matter?" he cried. "We didn't get any telegram from you; we were not expecting you till tomorrow."

Still his mother did not speak.

"Henriette was just going out," he exclaimed nervously; "I had better call her."

"No!" said his mother quickly. Her voice was low and trembling. "I did not want Henriette to be here when I arrived."

"But what's the matter?" cried George.

Again there was a silence before the reply came. He read something terrible in the mother's manner, and he found himself trembling violently.

"I have brought back the child and the nurse," said Madame Dupont.

"What! Is the little one sick?"

"Yes."

"What's the matter with her?"

47

"Nothing dangerous—for the moment, at least."

"We must send and get the doctor!" cried George.

"I have just come from the doctor's," was the reply. "He said it was necessary to take our child from the nurse and bring her up on the bottle."

Again there was a pause. George could hardly bring himself to ask the next question. Try as he would, he could not keep his voice from weakening. "Well, now, what is her trouble?"

The mother did not answer. She stood staring before her. At last she said, faintly, "I don't know."

"You didn't ask?"

"I asked. But it was not to our own doctor that I went."

"Ah!" whispered George. For nearly a minute neither one of them spoke. "Why?" he inquired at last.

"Because—he—the nurse's doctor—had frightened me so—"

"Truly?"

"Yes. It is a disease—" again she stopped.

George cried, in a voice of agony, "and then?"

"Then I asked him if the matter was so grave that I could not be satisfied with our ordinary doctor."

"And what did he answer?"

"He said that if we had the means it would really be better to consult a specialist."

George looked at his mother again. He was able to do it, because she was not looking at him. He clenched his hands and got himself together. "And—where did he send you?"

His mother fumbled in her hand bag and drew out a visiting card. "Here," she said.

And George looked at the card. It was all he could do to keep himself from tottering. It was the card of the doctor whom he had first consulted about his trouble! The specialist in venereal diseases!

CHAPTER IV

It was all George could do to control his voice. "You—you went to see him?" he stammered.

"Yes," said his mother. "You know him?"

"No, no," he answered. "Or—that is—I have met him, I think. I don't know." And then to himself, "My God!"

There was a silence. "He is coming to talk to you," said the mother, at last.

George was hardly able to speak. "Then he is very much disturbed?"

"No, but he wants to talk to you."

"To me?"

"Yes. When the doctor saw the nurse, he said, 'Madame, it is impossible for me to continue to attend this child unless I have had this very day a conversation with the father.' So I said 'Very well,' and he said he would come at once."

George turned away, and put his hands to his forehead. "My poor little daughter!" he whispered to himself.

"Yes," said the mother, her voice breaking, "she is, indeed, a poor little daughter!"

A silence fell; for what could words avail in such a situation? Hearing the door open, Madame Dupont started, for her nerves were all a-quiver with the strain she had been under. A servant came in and spoke to her, and she said to George, "It is the doctor. If you need me, I shall be in the next room."

Her son stood trembling, as if he were waiting the approach of an executioner. The other came into the room without seeing him and he stood for a minute, clasping and unclasping his hands, almost overcome with emotion. Then he said, "Good-day, doctor." As the man stared at him, surprised and puzzled, he added, "You don't recognize me?"

The doctor looked again, more closely. George was expecting him to break out in rage; but instead his voice fell low. "You!" he exclaimed. "It is you!"

At last, in a voice of discouragement than of anger, he went on, "You got married, and you have a child! After all that I told you! You are a wretch!"

"Sir," cried George, "let me explain to you!"

"Not a word!" exclaimed the other. "There can be no explanation for what you have done."

A silence followed. The young man did not know what to say. Finally, stretching out his arms, he pleaded, "You will take care of my little daughter all the same, will you not?"

The other turned away with disgust. "Imbecile!" he said.

George did not hear the word. "I was able to wait only six months," he murmured.

The doctor answered in a voice of cold self-repression, "That is enough, sir! All that does not concern me. I have done wrong even to let you see my indignation. I should have left you to judge yourself. I have nothing to do here but with the present and with the future—with the infant and with the nurse."

"She isn't in danger?" cried George.

"The nurse is in danger of being contaminated."

But George had not been thinking about the nurse. "I mean my child," he said.

"Just at present the symptoms are not disturbing."

George waited; after a while he began, "You were saying about the nurse. Will you consent that I call my mother? She knows better than I."

"As you wish," was the reply.

The young man started to the door, but came back, in terrible distress. "I have one prayer to offer you sir; arrange it so that my wife—so that no one will know. If my wife learned that it is I who am the cause—! It is for her that I implore you! She—she isn't to blame."

Said the doctor: "I will do everything in my power that she may be kept ignorant of the true nature of the disease."

"Oh, how I thank you!" murmured George. "How I thank you!"

"Do not thank me; it is for her, and not for you, that I will consent to lie."

"And my mother?"

"Your mother knows the truth."

"But—"

"I pray you, sir—we have enough to talk about, and very serious matters."

So George went to the door and called his mother. She entered and greeted the doctor, holding herself erect, and striving to keep the signs of grief and terror from her face. She signed to the doctor to take a seat, and then seated herself by a little table near him.

"Madame Dupont," he began, "I have prescribed a course of treatment for the child. I hope to be able to improve its condition, and to prevent any new developments. But my duty and yours does not stop there; if there is still time, it is necessary to protect the health of the nurse."

"Tell us what it is necessary to do, Doctor?" said she.

"The woman must stop nursing the child."

"You mean we have to change the nurse?"

"Madame, the child can no longer be brought up at the breast, either by that nurse or by any other nurse."

"But why, sir?"

"Because the child would give her disease to the woman who gave her milk."

"But, Doctor, if we put her on the bottle—our little one—she will die!"

And suddenly George burst out into sobs. "Oh, my poor little daughter! My God, my God!"

Said the doctor, "If the feeding is well attended to, with sterilized milk—"

"That can do very well for healthy infants," broke in Madame Dupont. "But at the age of three months one cannot take from the breast a baby like ours, frail and ill. More than any other such an infant has need of a nurse—is that not true?"

"Yes," the doctor admitted, "that is true. But—"

"In that case, between the life of the child, and the health of the nurse, you understand perfectly well that my choice is made."

Between her words the doctor heard the sobbing of George, whose head was buried in his arms. "Madame," he said, "your love for that baby has just caused you to utter something ferocious! It is not for you to choose. It is not for you to choose. I forbid the nursing. The health of that woman does not belong to you."

"No," cried the grandmother, wildly, "nor does the health of out child belong to you! If there is a hope of saving it, that hope is in giving it more care than any other child; and you would wish that I put it upon a mode of nourishment which the doctors condemn, even for vigorous infants! You expect that I will let myself be taken in like that? I answer you: she shall have the milk which she needs, my poor little one! If there was a single thing that one could do to save her—I should be a criminal to neglect it!" And Madame Dupont broke out, with furious scorn, "The nurse! The nurse! We shall know how to do our duty—we shall take care of her, repay her. But our child before all! No sir, no! Everything that can be done to save our baby I shall do, let it cost what it will. To do what you say—you don't realize it—it would be as if I should kill the child!" In the end the agonized woman burst into tears. "Oh, my poor little angel! My little savior!"

George had never ceased sobbing while his mother spoke; at these last words his sobs became loud cries. He struck the floor with his foot, he tore his hair, as if he were suffering from violent physical pain. "Oh, oh, oh!" he cried. "My little child! My little child!" And then, in a horrified whisper to himself, "I am a wretch! A criminal!"

"Madame," said the doctor, "you must calm yourself; you must both calm yourselves. You will not help out the situation by lamentations. You must learn to take it with calmness."

Madame Dupont set her lips together, and with a painful effort recovered her self-control. "You are right, sir," she said, in a low voice. "I ask your pardon; but if you only knew what that child means to me! I lost one at that age. I am an old woman, I am a widow—I had hardly hoped to live long enough to be a grandmother. But, as you say—we must be calm." She turned to the young man, "Calm yourself, my son. It is a poor way to show our love for the child, to abandon ourselves to tears. Let us talk, Doctor, and seriously—coldly. But I declare to you that nothing will ever induce me to put the child on the bottle, when I know that it might kill her. That is all I can say."

The doctor replied: "This isn't the first time that I find myself in the present situation. Madame, I declare to you that always—ALWAYS, you understand—persons who have rejected my advice have had reason to repent it cruelly."

"The only thing of which I should repent—" began the other.

"You simply do not know," interrupted the doctor, "what such a nurse is capable of. You cannot imagine what bitterness—legitimate bitterness, you understand—joined to the rapacity, the cupidity, the mischief-making impulse—might inspire these people to do. For them the BOURGEOIS is always somewhat of an enemy; and when they find themselves in position to avenge their inferiority, they are ferocious."

"But what could the woman do?"

"What could she do? She could bring legal proceedings against you."

"But she is much too stupid to have that idea."

"Others will put it into her mind."

"She is too poor to pay the preliminary expenses."

"And do you propose then to profit by her ignorance and stupidity? Besides, she could obtain judicial assistance."

"Why, surely," exclaimed Madame Dupont, "such a thing was never heard of! Do you mean that?"

"I know a dozen prosecutions of that sort; and always when there has been certainty, the parents have lost their case."

"But surely, Doctor, you must be mistaken! Not in a case like ours—not when it is a question of saving the life of a poor little innocent!"

"Oftentimes exactly such facts have been presented."

Here George broke in. "I can give you the dates of the decisions."
He rose from his chair, glad of an opportunity to be useful. "I have
the books," he said, and took one from the case and brought it to
the doctor.

"All of that is no use—" interposed the mother.

But the doctor said to George, "You will be able to convince
yourself. The parents have been forced once or twice to pay the
nurse a regular income, and at other times they have had to pay her
an indemnity, of which the figure has varied between three and
eight thousand francs."

Madame Dupont was ready with a reply to this. "Never fear, sir! If
there should be a suit, we should have a good lawyer. We shall be
able to pay and choose the best—and he would demand, without
doubt, which of the two, the nurse or the child, has given the
disease to the other."

The doctor was staring at her in horror. "Do you not perceive that
would be a monstrous thing to do?"

"Oh, I would not have to say it," was the reply. "The lawyer would
see to it—is not that his profession? My point is this: by one means
or another he would make us win our case."

"And the scandal that would result," replied the other. "Have you
thought of that?"

Here George, who had been looking over his law-books, broke in.
"Doctor, permit me to give you a little information. In cases of this
sort, the names are never printed."

"Yes, but they are spoken at the hearings."

"That's true."

"And are you certain that there will not be any newspaper to print
the judgment?"

"What won't they stoop to," exclaimed Madame Dupont—"those filthy journals!"

"Ah," said the other, "and see what a scandal? What a shame it would be to you!"

"The doctor is right, mother," exclaimed the young man.

But Madame Dupont was not yet convinced. "We will prevent the woman from taking any steps; we will give her what she demands from us."

"But then," said the other, "you will give yourselves up to the risk of blackmail. I know a family which has been thus held up for over twelve years."

"If you will permit me, Doctor," said George, timidly, "she could be made to sign a receipt."

"For payment in full?" asked the doctor, scornfully.

"Even so."

"And then," added his mother, "she would be more than delighted to go back to her country with a full purse. She would be able to buy a little house and a bit of ground—in that country one doesn't need so much in order to live."

At this moment there was a tap upon the door, and the nurse entered. She was a country woman, robust, rosy-cheeked, fairly bursting with health. When she spoke one got the impression that her voice was more than she could contain. It did not belong in a drawing-room, but under the open sky of her country home. "Sir," she said, addressing the doctor, "the baby is awake."

"I will go and see her," was the reply; and then to Madame Dupont, "We will take up this conversation later on."

"Certainly," said the mother. "Will you have need of the nurse?"

"No, Madame," the doctor answered.

"Nurse," said the mother, "sit down and rest. Wait a minute, I wish to speak to you." As the doctor went out, she took her son to one side and whispered to him, "I know the way to arrange everything. If we let her know what is the matter, and if she accepts, the doctor will have nothing more to say. Isn't that so?"

"Obviously," replied the son.

"I am going to promise that we will give her two thousand francs when she goes away, if she will consent to continue nursing the child."

"Two thousand francs?" said the other. "Is that enough?"

"I will see," was the reply. "If she hesitates, I will go further. Let me attend to it."

George nodded his assent, and Madame Dupont returned to the nurse. "You know," she said, "that our child is a little sick?"

The other looked at her in surprise. "Why no, ma'am!"

"Yes," said the grandmother.

"But, ma'am, I have taken the best of care of her; I have always kept her proper."

"I am not saying anything to the contrary," said Madame Dupont, "but the child is sick, the doctors have said it."

The nurse was not to be persuaded; she thought they were getting ready to scold her. "Humph," she said, "that's a fine thing—the doctors! If they couldn't always find something wrong you'd say they didn't know their business."

"But our doctor is a great doctor; and you have seen yourself that our child has some little pimples."

58

"Ah, ma'am," said the nurse, "that's the heat—it's nothing but the heat of the blood breaking out. You don't need to bother yourself; I tell you it's only the child's blood. It's not my fault; I swear to you that she had not lacked anything, and that I have always kept her proper."

"I am not reproaching you—"

"What is there to reproach me for? Oh, what bad luck! She's tiny—the little one—she's a bit feeble; but Lord save us, she's a city child! And she's getting along all right, I tell you."

"No," persisted Madame Dupont, "I tell you—she has got a cold in her head, and she has an eruption at the back of the throat."

"Well," cried the nurse, angrily, "if she has, it's because the doctor scratched her with that spoon he put into her mouth wrong end first! A cold in the head? Yes, that's true; but if she has caught cold, I can't say when, I don't know anything about it—nothing, nothing at all. I have always kept her well covered; she's always had as much as three covers on her. The truth is, it was when you came, the time before last; you were all the time insisting upon opening the windows in the house!"

"But once more I tell you," cried Madame Dupont, "we are not putting any blame on you."

"Yes," cried the woman, more vehemently. "I know what that kind of talk means. It's no use—when you're a poor country woman."

"What are you imagining now?" demanded the other.

"Oh, that's all right. It's no use when you're a poor country woman."

"I repeat to you once more," cried Madame Dupont, with difficulty controlling her impatience, "we have nothing whatever to blame you for."

But the nurse began to weep. "If I had known that anything like this was coming to me—"

"We have nothing to blame you for," declared the other. "We only wish to warn you that you might possibly catch the disease of the child."

The woman pouted. "A cold in the head!" she exclaimed. "Well, if I catch it, it won't be the first time. I know how to blow my nose."

"But you might also get the pimples."

At this the nurse burst into laughter so loud that the bric-a-brac rattled. "Oh, oh, oh! Dear lady, let me tell you, we ain't city folks, we ain't; we don't have such soft skins. What sort of talk is that? Pimples—what difference would that make to poor folks like us? We don't have a white complexion like the ladies of Paris. We are out all day in the fields, in the sun and the rain, instead of rubbing cold cream on our muzzles! No offense, ma'am—but I say if you're looking for an excuse to get rid of me, you must get a better one than that."

"Excuse!" exclaimed the other. "What in the world do you mean?"

"Oh, I know!" said the nurse, nodding her head.

"But speak!"

"It's no use, when you're only a poor country woman."

"I don't understand you! I swear to you that I don't understand you!"

"Well," sneered the other, "I understand."

"But then—explain yourself."

"No, I don't want to say it."

"But you must; I wish it."

"Well—"

"Go ahead."

"I'm only a poor country woman, but I am no more stupid than the others, for all that. I know perfectly well what your tricks mean. Mr. George here has been grumbling because you promised me thirty francs more a month, if I came to Paris." And then, turning upon the other, she went on—"But, sir, isn't it only natural? Don't I have to put my own child away somewheres else? And then, can my husband live on his appetite? We're nothing but poor country people, we are."

"You are making a mistake, nurse," broke in George. "It is nothing at all of that sort; mother is quite right. I am so far from wanting to reproach you, that, on the contrary, I think she had not promised enough, and I want to make you, for my part, another promise. When you go away, when baby is old enough to be weaned, by way of thanking you, we wish to give you—"

Madame Dupont broke in, hurriedly, "We wish to give you,—over and above your wages, you understand—we wish to give you five hundred francs, and perhaps a thousand, if the little one is altogether in good health. You understand?"

The nurse stared at her, stupefied. "You will give me five hundred francs—for myself?" She sought to comprehend the words. "But that was not agreed, you don't have to do that at all."

"No," admitted Madame Dupont.

"But then," whispered the nurse, half to herself, "that's not natural."

"Yes," the other hurried on, "it is because the baby will have need of extra care. You will have to take more trouble; you will have to give it medicines; your task will be a little more delicate, a little more difficult."

"Oh, yes; then it's so that I will be sure to take care of her? I understand."

"Then it's agreed?" exclaimed Madame Dupont, with relief.

"Yes ma'am," said the nurse.

"And you won't come later on to make reproaches to us? We understand one another clearly? We have warned you that the child is sick and that you could catch the disease. Because of that, because of the special need of care which she has, we promise you five hundred francs at the end of the nursing. That's all right, is it?

"But, my lady," cried the nurse, all her cupidity awakened, "you spoke just now of a thousand francs."

"Very well, then, a thousand francs."

George passed behind the nurse and got his mother by the arm, drawing her to one side. "It would be a mistake," he whispered, "if we did not make her sign an agreement to all that."

His mother turned to the nurse. "In order that there may be no misunderstanding about the sum—you see how it is, I had forgotten already that I had spoken of a thousand francs—we will draw up a little paper, and you, on your part, will write one for us."

"Very good, ma'am," said the nurse, delighted with the idea of so important a transaction. "Why, it's just as you do when you rent a house!"

"Here comes the doctor," said the other. "Come, nurse, it is agreed?"

"Yes, ma'am," was the answer. But all the same, as she went out she hesitated and looked sharply first at the doctor, and then at George and his mother. She suspected that something was wrong, and she meant to find out if she could.

The doctor seated himself in George's office chair, as if to write a prescription. "The child's condition remains the same," he said; "nothing disturbing."

"Doctor," said Madame Dupont, gravely, "from now on, you will be able to devote your attention to the baby and the nurse without any scruple. During your absence we have arranged matters nicely. The nurse has been informed about the situation, and she does not mind. She has agreed to accept an indemnity, and the amount has been stated."

But the doctor did not take these tidings as the other had hoped he might. He replied: "The malady which the nurse will almost inevitably contract in feeding the child is too grave in its consequences. Such consequences might go as far as complete helplessness, even as far as death. So I say that the indemnity, whatever it might be, would not pay the damage."

"But," exclaimed the other, "she accepts it! She is mistress of herself, and she has the right—"

"I am not at all certain that she has the right to sell her own health. And I am certain that she has not the right to sell the health of her husband and her children. If she becomes infected, it is nearly certain that she will communicate the disease to them; the health and the life of the children she might have later on would be greatly compromised. Such things she cannot possibly sell. Come, madame, you must see that a bargain of this sort isn't possible. If the evil has not been done, you must do everything to avoid it."

"Sir," protested the mother, wildly, "you do not defend our interests!"

"Madame," was the reply, "I defend those who are weakest."

"If we had called in our own physician, who knows us," she protested, "he would have taken sides with us."

The doctor rose, with a severe look on his face. "I doubt it," he said, "but there is still time to call him."

George broke in with a cry of distress. "Sir, I implore you!"

And the mother in turn cried. "Don't abandon us, sir! You ought to make allowances! If you knew what that child is to me! I tell you it seems to me as if I had waited for her coming in order to die. Have pity upon us! Have pity upon her! You speak of the weakest—it is not she who is the weakest? You have seen her, you have seen that poor little baby, so emaciated! You have seen what a heap of suffering she is already; and cannot that inspire in you any sympathy? I pray you, sir—I pray you!"

"I pity her," said the doctor, "I would like to save her—and I will do everything for her. But do not ask me to sacrifice to a feeble infant, with an uncertain and probably unhappy life, the health of a sound and robust woman. It is useless for us to continue such a discussion as that."

Whereupon Madame Dupont leaped up in sudden frenzy. "Very Well!" she exclaimed. "I will not follow your counsels, I will not listen to you!"

Said the doctor in a solemn voice: "There is already some one here who regrets that he did not listen to me."

"Yes," moaned George, "to my misfortune, to the misfortune of all of us."

But Madame Dupont was quite beside herself. "Very well!" she cried. "If it is a fault, if it is a crime, if I shall have to suffer remorse for it in this life, and all the punishments in the life to come—I accept it all for myself alone! Myself alone, I take that responsibility! It is frightfully heavy, but I accept it. I am profoundly a Christian sir; I believe in eternal damnation; but to save my little child I consent to lose my soul forever. Yes, my mind is made up—I will do everything to save that life! Let God judge me; and if he condemns me, so much the worse for me!"

The doctor answered: "That responsibility is one which I cannot let you take, for it will be necessary that I should accept my part, and I refuse it."

"What will you do?"

"I shall warn the nurse. I shall inform her exactly, completely—something which you have not done, I feel sure."

"What?" cried Madame Dupont, wildly. "You, a doctor, called into a family which gives you its entire confidence, which hands over to you its most terrible secrets, its most horrible miseries—you would betray them?"

"It is not a betrayal," replied the man, sternly. "It is something which the law commands; and even if the law were silent, I would not permit a family of worthy people to go astray so far as to commit a crime. Either I give up the case, or you have the nursing of the child stopped."

"You threaten! You threaten!" cried the woman, almost frantic. "You abuse the power which your knowledge gives you! You know that it is you whose attention we need by that little cradle; you know that we believe in you, and you threaten to abandon us! Your abandonment means the death of the child, perhaps! And if I listen to you, if we stop the nursing of the child—that also means her death!"

She flung up her hands like a mad creature. "And yet there is no other means! Ah, my God! Why do you not let it be possible for me to sacrifice myself? I would wish nothing more than to be able to do it—if only you might take my old body, my old flesh, my old bones—if only I might serve for something! How quickly would I consent that it should infect me—this atrocious malady! How I would offer myself to it—with what joys, with what delights—however disgusting, however frightful it might be, however much to be dreaded! Yes, I would take it without fear, without regret, if my poor old empty breasts might still give to the child the milk which would preserve its life!"

She stopped; and George sprang suddenly from his seat, and fled to her and flung himself down upon his knees before her, mingling his sobs and tears with hers.

The doctor rose and moved about the room, unable any longer to control his distress. "Oh, the poor people!" he murmured to himself. "The poor, poor people!"

The storm passed, and Madame Dupont, who was a woman of strong character, got herself together. Facing the doctor again, she said, "Come, sir, tell us what we have to do."

"You must stop the nursing, and keep the woman here as a dry nurse, in order that she may not go away to carry the disease elsewhere. Do not exaggerate to yourself the danger which will result to the child. I am, in truth, extremely moved by your suffering, and I will do everything—I swear it to you—that your baby may recover as quickly as possible its perfect health. I hope to succeed, and that soon. And now I must leave you until tomorrow."

"Thank you, Doctor, thank you," said Madame Dupont, faintly.

The young man rose and accompanied the doctor to the door. He could not bring himself to speak, but stood hanging his head until the other was gone. Then he came to his mother. He sought to embrace her, but she repelled him—without violence, but firmly.

Her son stepped back and put his hands over his face. "Forgive me!" he said, in a broken voice. "Are we not unhappy enough, without hating each other?"

His mother answered: "God has punished you for your debauch by striking at your child."

But, grief-stricken as the young man was, he could not believe that. "Impossible!" he said. "There is not even a man sufficiently wicked or unjust to commit the act which you attribute to your God!"

"Yes," said his mother, sadly, "you believe in nothing."

"I believe in no such God as that," he answered.

A silence followed. When it was broken, it was by the entrance of the nurse. She had opened the door of the room and had been standing there for some moments, unheeded. Finally she stepped forward. "Madame," she said, "I have thought it over; I would rather go back to my home at once, and have only the five hundred francs."

Madame Dupont stared at her in consternation. "What is that you are saying? You want to return to your home?"

"Yes, ma'am," was the answer.

"But," cried George, "only ten minutes ago you were not thinking of it."

"What has happened since then?" demanded Madame Dupont.

"I have thought it over."

"Thought it over?"

"Well, I am getting lonesome for my little one and for my husband."

"In the last ten minutes?" exclaimed George.

"There must be something else," his mother added. "Evidently there must be something else."

"No!" insisted the nurse.

"But I say yes!"

"Well, I'm afraid the air of Paris might not be good for me."

"You had better wait and try it."

"I would rather go back at once to my home."

"Come, now," cried Madame Dupont, "tell us why?"

"I have told you. I have thought it over."

"Thought what over?"

"Well, I have thought."

"Oh," cried the mother, "what a stupid reply! 'I have thought it over! I have thought it over!' Thought WHAT over, I want to know!"

"Well, everything."

"Don't you know how to tell us what?"

"I tell you, everything."

"Why," exclaimed Madame Dupont, "you are an imbecile!"

George stepped between his mother and the nurse. "Let me talk to her," he said.

The woman came back to her old formula: "I know that we're only poor country people."

"Listen to me, nurse," said the young man. "Only a little while ago you were afraid that we would send you away. You were satisfied with the wages which my mother had fixed. In addition to those wages we had promised you a good sum when you returned to your home. Now you tell us that you want to go away. You see? All at once. There must be some reason; let us understand it. There must certainly be a reason. Has anybody done anything to you?"

"No, sir," said the woman, dropping her eyes.

"Well, then?"

"I have thought it over."

George burst out, "Don't go on repeating always the same thing—'I have thought it over!' That's not telling us anything." Controlling himself, he added, gently, "Come, tell me why you want to go away?"

There was a silence. "Well?" he demanded.

"I tell you, I have thought—"

George exclaimed in despair, "It's as if one were talking to a block of wood!"

His mother took up the conversation again. "You must realize, you have not the right to go away."

The woman answered, "I WANT to go."

"But I will not let you leave us."

"No," interrupted George angrily, "let her go; we cannot fasten her here."

"Very well, then," cried the exasperated mother, "since you want to go, go! But I have certainly the right to say to you that you are as stupid as the animals on your farm!"

"I don't say that I am not," answered the woman.

"I will not pay you the month which has just begun, and you will pay your railroad fare for yourself."

The other drew back with a look of anger. "Oho!" she cried. "We'll see about that!"

"Yes, we'll see about it!" cried George. "And you will get out of here at once. Take yourself off—I will have no more to do with you. Good evening."

"No, George," protested his mother, "don't lose control of yourself." And then, with a great effort at calmness, "That cannot be serious, nurse! Answer me."

"I would rather go off right away to my home, and only have my five hundred francs."

"WHAT?" cried George, in consternation.

"What's that you are telling me?" exclaimed Madame Dupont.

"Five hundred francs?" repeated her son.

"What five hundred francs?" echoed the mother.

"The five hundred francs you promised me," said the nurse.

"We have promised you five hundred francs? WE?"

"Yes."

"When the child should be weaned, and if we should be satisfied with you! That was our promise."

"No. You said you would give them to me when I was leaving. Now I am leaving, and I want them."

Madame Dupont drew herself up, haughtily. "In the first place," she said, "kindly oblige me by speaking to me in another tone; do you understand?"

The woman answered, "You have nothing to do but give me my money, and I will say nothing more."

George went almost beside himself with rage at this. "Oh, it's like that?" he shouted. "Very well; I'll show you!" And he sprang to the door and opened it.

But the nurse never budged. "Give me my five hundred francs!" she said.

George seized her by the arm and shoved her toward the door. "You clear out of here, do you understand me? And as quickly as you can!"

The woman shook her arm loose, and sneered into his face. "Come now, you—you can talk to me a little more politely, eh?"

"Will you go?" shouted George, completely beside himself. "Will you go, or must I go out and look for a policeman?"

"A policeman!" demanded the woman. "For what?"

"To put you outside! You are behaving yourself like a thief."

"A thief? I? What do you mean?"

"I mean that you are demanding money which doesn't belong to you."

"More than that," broke in Madame Dupont, "you are destroying that poor little baby! You are a wicked woman!"

"I will put you out myself!" shouted George, and seized her by the arm again.

"Oh, it's like that, is it?" retorted the nurse. "Then you really want me to tell you why I am going away?"

"Yes, tell me!" cried he.

His mother added, "Yes, yes!"

She would have spoken differently had she chanced to look behind her and seen Henriette, who at that moment appeared in the doorway. She had been about to go out, when her attention had been caught by the loud voices. She stood now, amazed, clasping her hands together, while the nurse, shaking her fist first at Madame Dupont and then at her son, cried loudly, "Very well! I'm going away because I don't want to catch a filthy disease here!"

"HUSH!" cried Madame Dupont, and sprang toward her, her hands clenched as if she would choke her.

"Be silent!" cried George, wild with terror.

But the woman rushed on without dropping her voice, "Oh, you need not be troubling yourselves for fear anyone should overhear! All the world knows it! Your other servants were listening with me at your door! They heard every word your doctor said!"

"Shut up!" screamed George.

Her mother seized the woman fiercely by the arm. "Hold your tongue!" she hissed.

But again the other shook herself loose. She was powerful, and now her rage was not to be controlled. She waved her hands in the air, shouting, "Let me be, let me be! I know all about your brat—that you will never be able to raise it—that it's rotten because it's father has a filthy disease he got from a woman of the street!"

She got no farther. She was interrupted by a frenzied shriek from Henriette. The three turned, horrified, just in time to see her fall forward upon the floor, convulsed.

"My God!" cried George. He sprang toward her, and tried to lift her, but she shrank from him, repelling him with a gesture of disgust, of hatred, of the most profound terror. "Don't touch me!" she screamed, like a maniac. "Don't touch me!"

CHAPTER V

It was in vain that Madame Dupont sought to control her daughter-in-law. Henriette was beside herself, frantic, she could not be brought to listen to any one. She rushed into the other room, and when the older woman followed her, shrieked out to be left alone. Afterwards, she fled to her own room and barred herself in, and George and his mother waited distractedly for hours until she should give some sign.

Would she kill herself, perhaps? Madame Dupont hovered on guard about the door of the nursery for fear that the mother in her fit of insanity might attempt some harm to her child.

The nurse had slunk away abashed when she saw the consequences of her outburst. By the time she had got her belongings packed, she had recovered her assurance. She wanted her five hundred; also she wanted her wages and her railroad fare home. She wanted them at once, and she would not leave until she got them. George and his mother, in the midst of all their anguish of mind, had to go through a disgusting scene with this coarse and angry woman.

They had no such sum of money in the house, and the nurse refused to accept a check. She knew nothing about a check. It was so much paper, and might be some trick that they were playing on her. She kept repeating her old formula, "I am nothing but a poor country woman." Nor would she be contented with the promise that she would receive the money the next day. She seemed to be afraid that if she left the house she would be surrendering her claim. So at last the distracted George to sally forth and obtain the cash from some tradesmen in the neighborhood.

The woman took her departure. They made her sign a receipt in full for all claims and they strove to persuade themselves that this made them safe; but in their hearts they had no real conviction of safety. What was the woman's signature, or her pledged word, against the cupidity of her husband and relatives. Always she would have the dreadful secret to hold over them, and so they would live under the shadow of possible blackmail.

Later in the day Henriette sent for her mother-in-law. She was white, her eyes were swollen with weeping, and she spoke in a voice choked with sobs. She wished to return at once to her father's home, and to take little Gervaise with her. Madame Dupont cried out in horror at this proposition, and argued and pleaded and wept—but all to no purpose. The girl was immovable. She would not stay under her husband's roof, and she would take her child with her. It was her right, and no one could refuse her.

The infant had been crying for hours, but that made no difference. Henriette insisted that a cab should be called at once.

So she went back to the home of Monsieur Loches and told him the hideous story. Never before in her life had she discussed such subjects with any one, but now in her agitation she told her father all. As George had declared to the doctor, Monsieur Loches was a person of violent temper; at this revelation, at the sight of his daughter's agony, he was almost beside himself. His face turned purple, the veins stood out on his forehead; a trembling seized him. He declared that he would kill George—there was nothing else to do. Such a scoundrel should not be permitted to live.

The effort which Henriette had to make to restrain him had a calming effect upon herself. Bitter and indignant as she was, she did not want George to be killed. She clung to her father, beseeching him to promise her that he would not do such a thing; and all that day and evening she watched him, unwilling to let him out of her sight.

There was a matter which claimed her immediate attention, and which helped to withdraw them from the contemplation of their own sufferings. The infant must be fed and cared for—the unhappy victim of other people's sins, whose life was now imperiled. A dry nurse must be found at once, a nurse competent to take every precaution and give the child every chance. This nurse must be informed of the nature of the trouble—another matter which required a great deal of anxious thought.

That evening came Madame Dupont, tormented by anxiety about the child's welfare, and beseeching permission to help take care of it. It was impossible to refuse such a request. Henriette could not endure to see her, but the poor grandmother would come and sit for hours in the nursery, watching the child and the nurse, in silent agony.

This continued for days, while poor George wandered about at home, suffering such torment of mind as can hardly be imagined. Truly, in these days he paid for his sins; he paid a thousand-fold in agonized and impotent regret. He looked back upon the course of his life, and traced one by one the acts which had led him and those he loved into this nightmare of torment. He would have been willing to give his life if he could have undone those acts. But avenging nature offered him no such easy deliverance as that. We shudder as we read the grim words of the Jehovah of the ancient Hebrews; and yet not all the learning of modern times has availed to deliver us from the cruel decree, that the sins of the fathers shall be visited upon the children.

George wrote notes to his wife, imploring her forgiveness. He poured out all his agony and shame to her, begging her to see him just once, to give him a chance to plead his defense. It was not much of a defense, to be sure; it was only that he had done no worse than the others did—only that he was a wretched victim of ignorance. But he loved her, he had proven that he loved her, and he pleaded that for the sake of their child she would forgive him.

When all this availed nothing, he went to see the doctor, whose advice he had so shamefully neglected. He besought this man to intercede for him—which the doctor, of course, refused to do. It was an extra-medical matter, he said, and George was absurd to expect him to meddle in it.

But, as a matter of fact, the doctor had already been interceding—he had gone farther in pleading George's cause than he was willing to have George know. For Monsieur Loches had paid him a visit—his purpose being to ask the doctor to continue attendance upon the infant, and also to give Henriette a certificate which she could use in her suit for a divorce from her husband.

So inevitably there had been a discussion of the whole question between the two men. The doctor had granted the first request, but refused the second. In the first place, he said, there was a rule of professional secrecy which would prevent him. And when the father-in-law requested to know if the rule of professional secrecy compelled him to protect a criminal against honest people, the doctor answered that even if his ethics permitted it, he would still refuse the request. "I would reproach myself forever," he said, "if I had aided you to obtain such a divorce."

"Then," cried the old man, vehemently, "because you profess such and such theories, because the exercise of your profession makes you the constant witness of such miseries—therefore it is necessary that my daughter should continue to bear that man's name all her life!"

The doctor answered, gently, "Sir, I understand and respect your grief. But believe me, you are not in a state of mind to decide about these matters now."

"You are mistaken," declared the other, controlling himself with an effort. "I have been thinking about nothing else for days. I have discussed it with my daughter, and she agrees with me. Surely, sir, you cannot desire that my daughter should continue to live with a man who has struck her so brutal, so cowardly, a blow."

"If I refuse your request," the doctor answered, "it is in the interest of your daughter." Then, seeing the other's excitement returning, he continued, "In your state of mind, Monsieur Loches, I know that you will probably be abusing me before five minutes has passed. But that will not trouble me. I have seen many cases. And since I have made the mistake of letting myself be trapped into this discussion, I must explain to you the reason for my attitude. You ask of me a certificate so that you may prove in court that your son-in-law is afflicted with syphilis."

"Precisely," said the other.

"And have you not reflected upon this—that at the same time you will be publicly attesting that your daughter has been exposed to the contagion? With such an admission, an admission officially registered in the public records, do you believe that she will find it easy to re-marry later on?"

"She will never re-marry," said the father.

"She says that today, but can you affirm that she will say the same thing five years from now, ten years from now? I tell you you will not obtain that divorce, because I will most certainly refuse you the necessary certificate."

"Then," cried the other, "I will find other means of establishing proofs. I will have the child examined by another doctor!"

The other answered. "Then you do not find that that poor little one has been already sufficiently handicapped at the outset of its life? Your granddaughter has a physical defect. Do you wish to add to that a certificate of hereditary syphilis, which will follow her all her life?"

Monsieur Loches sprang from his chair. "You mean that if the victims seek to defend themselves, they will be struck the harder! You mean that the law gives me no weapon against a man who, knowing his condition, takes a young girl, sound, trusting, innocent, and befouls her with the result of his debauches—makes her the mother of a poor little creature, whose future is such that those who love her the most do not know whether they ought to pray for her life, or for her immediate deliverance? Sir," he continued, in his orator's voice, "that man has inflicted upon the woman he has married a supreme insult. He has made her the victim of the most odious assault. He has degraded her—he has brought her, so to speak, into contact with the woman of the streets. He has created between her and that common woman I know not what mysterious relationship. It is the poisoned blood of the prostitute which poisons my daughter and her child; that abject creature, she lives, she lives in us! She belongs to our family—he has given her a seat at our hearth! He has soiled the imagination and the thoughts of my poor child, as he has soiled her body. He has united forever in her soul the idea of love which she has placed so high, with I know not what horrors of the hospitals. He has tainted her in her dignity and her modesty, in her love as well as in her baby. He has struck her down with physical and moral decay, he has overwhelmed her with vileness. And yet the law is such, the customs of society are such, that the woman cannot separate herself from that man save by the aid of legal proceedings whose scandal will fall upon herself and upon her child!"

Monsieur Loches had been pacing up and down the room as he spoke, and now he clenched his fists in sudden fury.

"Very well! I will not address myself to the law. Since I learned the truth I have been asking myself if it was not my duty to find that monster and to put a bullet into his head, as one does to a mad dog. I don't know what weakness, what cowardice, has held me back, and decided me to appeal to the law. Since the law will not protect me, I will seek justice for myself. Perhaps his death will be a good warning for the others!"

The doctor shrugged his shoulders, as if to say that this was no affair of his and that he would not try to interfere. But he remarked, quietly: "You will be tried for your life."

"I shall be acquitted!" cried the other.

"Yes, but after a public revelation of all your miseries. You will make the scandal greater, the miseries greater—that is all. And how do you know but that on the morrow of your acquittal, you will find yourself confronting another court, a higher and more severe one? How do you know but that your daughter, seized at last by pity for the man you have killed, will not demand to know by what right you have acted so, by what right you have made an orphan of her child? How can you know but that her child also may some day demand an accounting of you?"

Monsieur Loches let his hands fall, and stood, a picture of crushed despair. "Tell me then," he said, in a faint voice, "what ought I to do?"

"Forgive!"

For a while the doctor sat looking at him. "Sir," he said, at last, "tell me one thing. You are inflexible; you feel you have the right to be inflexible. But are you really so certain that it was not your duty, once upon a time, to save your daughter from the possibility of such misfortune?"

"What?" cried the other. "My duty? What do you mean?"

"I mean this, sir. When that marriage was being discussed, you certainly took precautions to inform yourself about the financial condition of your future son-in-law. You demanded that he should prove to you that his stocks and bonds were actual value, listed on the exchange. Also, you obtained some information about his character. In fact, you forgot only one point, the most important of all—that was, to inquire if he was in good health. You never did that."

The father-in-law's voice had become faint. "No," he said.

"But why not?"

"Because that is not the custom."

"Very well, but that ought to be the custom. Surely the father of a

79

family, before he gives his daughter to a man, should take as much precaution as a business concern which accepts an employee."

"You are right," was the reply, "there should be a law." The man spoke as a deputy, having authority in these matters.

But the doctor cried, "No, no, sir! Do not make a new law. We have too many already. There is no need of it. It would suffice that people should know a little better what syphilis is. The custom would establish itself very quickly for a suitor to add to all the other documents which he presents, a certificate of a doctor, as proof that he could be received into a family without bringing a pestilence with him. That would be very simple. Once let the custom be established, then the suitor would go to the doctor for a certificate of health, just as he goes to the priest for a certificate that he has confessed; and by that means you would prevent a great deal of suffering in the world. Or let me put it another way, sir. Nowadays, before you conclude a marriage, you get the lawyers of the two families together. It would be of at least equal importance to get their two doctors together. You see, sir, your inquiry concerning your son-in-law was far from complete. So your daughter may fairly ask you, why you, being a man, being a father who ought to know these things, did not take as much care of her health as you took of her fortune. So it is, sir, that I say to you, forgive!"

But Monsieur Loches said again, "Never!"

And again the doctor sat and watched him for a minute. "Come, sir," he began, finally, "since it is necessary to employ the last argument, I will do so. To be so severe and so pitiless—are you yourself without sin?"

The other answered, "I have never had a shameful disease."

"I do not ask you that," interrupted the doctor. "I ask you if you have never exposed yourself to the chance of having it." And then, reading the other's face, he went on, in a tone of quiet certainty. "Yes, you have exposed yourself. Then, sir, it was not virtue that you had; it was good fortune. That is one of the things which exasperate me the most—that term 'shameful disease' which you have just used. Like all other diseases, that is one of our misfortunes, and it is never shameful to be unfortunate—even if one has deserved it." The doctor paused, and then with some excitement he went on: "Come, sir, come, we must understand each other. Among men the most exacting, among those who with their middle-class prudery dare not pronounce the name of syphilis, or who make the most terrifying faces, the most disgusted, when they consent to speak of it—who regard the syphilitic as sinners—I should wish to know how many there are who have never exposed themselves to a similar misadventure. They and they alone have the right to speak. How many are there? Among a thousand men, are there four? Very well, then. Excepting those four, between all the rest and the syphilitic there is nothing but the difference of chance."

There came into the doctor's voice at this moment a note of intense feeling; for these were matters of which evidence came to him every day. "I tell you, sir, that such people are deserving of sympathy, because they are suffering. If they have committed a fault, they have at least the plea that they are expiating it. No, sir, let me hear no more of that hypocrisy. Recall your own youth, sir. That which afflicts your son-in-law, you have deserved it just as much as he— more than he, perhaps. Therefore, have pity on him; have for him the toleration which the unpunished criminal ought to have for the criminal less fortunate than himself upon whom the penalty has fallen. Is that not so?"

Monsieur Loches had been listening to this discourse with the feeling of a thief before the bar. There was nothing that he could answer. "Sir," he stammered, "as you present this thing to me—"

"But am I not right?" insisted the doctor.

"Perhaps you are," the other admitted. "But—I cannot say all that to my daughter, to persuade her to go back to her husband."

"You can give her other arguments," was the answer.

"What arguments, in God's name?"

"There is no lack of them. You will say to her that a separation would be a misfortune for all; that her husband is the only one in the world who would be devoted enough to help her save her child. You will say to her that out of the ruins of her first happiness she can build herself another structure, far stronger. And, sir, you will add to that whatever your good heart may suggest—and we will arrange so that the next child of the pair shall be sound and vigorous."

Monsieur Loches received this announcement with the same surprise that George himself had manifested. "Is that possible?" he asked.

The doctor cried: "Yes, yes, yes—a thousand times yes! There is a phrase which I repeat on every occasion, and which I would wish to post upon the walls. It is that syphilis is an imperious mistress, who only demands that one should recognize her power. She is terrible for those who think her insignificant, and gentle with those who know how dangerous she is. You know that kind of mistress— who is only vexed when she is neglected. You may tell this to your daughter—you will restore her to the arms of her husband, from whom she has no longer anything to fear, and I will guarantee that you will be a happy grandfather two years from now."

Monsieur Loches at last showed that he was weakened in his resolution.

"Doctor," he said, "I do not know that I can ever go so far as forgiveness, but I promise you that I will do no irreparable act, and that I will not oppose a reconciliation if after the lapse of some time—I cannot venture to say how long—my poor child should make up her mind to a reconciliation."

"Very good," said the other. "But let me add this: If you have another daughter, take care to avoid the fault which you committed when you married off the first."

"But," said the old man, "I did not know."

"Ah, surely!" cried the other. "You did not know! You are a father, and you did not know! You are a deputy, you have assumed the responsibility and the honor of making our laws—and you did not know! You are ignorant about syphilis, just as you probably are ignorant about alcoholism and tuberculosis."

"No," exclaimed the other, quickly.

"Very well," said the doctor, "I will leave you out, if you wish. I am talking of the others, the five hundred, and I don't know how many more, who are there in the Chamber of Deputies, and who call themselves representatives of the people. They are not able to find a single hour to discuss these three cruel gods, to which egotism and indifference make every day such frightful human sacrifices. They have not sufficient leisure to combat this ferocious trinity, which destroys every day thousands of lives. Alcoholism! It would be necessary to forbid the manufacture of poisons, and to restrict the number of licenses; but as one has fear of the great distillers, who are rich and powerful, and of the little dealers, who are the masters of universal suffrage, one puts one's conscience to sleep by lamenting the immorality of the working-class, and publishing little pamphlets and sermons. Imbeciles!...Tuberculosis! Everybody knows the true remedy, which would be the paying of sufficient wages, and the tearing down of the filthy tenements into which the laborers are packed—those who are the most useful and the most unfortunate among our population! But needless to say, no one wants that remedy, so we go round begging the workingmen not to spit on the sidewalks. Wonderful! But syphilis—why do you not occupy yourself with that? Why, since you have ministers whose duty it is to attend to all sorts of things, do you not have a minister to attend to the public health?"

"My dear Doctor," responded Monsieur Loches, "you fall into the French habit of considering the government as the cause of all evils. Show us the way, you learned gentlemen! Since that is a matter about which you are informed, and we are ignorant, begin by telling us what measures you believe to be necessary."

"Ah, ah!" exclaimed the other. "That's fine, indeed! It was about eighteen years ago that a project of that nature, worked out by the Academy of Medicine, and approved by it UNANIMOUSLY, was sent to the proper minister. We have not yet heard his reply."

"You really believe," inquired Monsieur Loches, in some bewilderment, "you believe that there are some measures—"

"Sir," broke in the doctor, "before we get though, you are going to suggest some measures yourself. Let me tell you what happened today. When I received your card I did not know that you were the father-in-law of George Dupont. I say that you were a deputy, and I thought that you wanted to get some information about these matters. There was a woman patient waiting to see me, and I kept her in my waiting-room—saying to myself, This is just the sort of person that our deputies ought to talk to."

The doctor paused for a moment, then continued: "Be reassured, I will take care of your nerves. This patient has no trouble that is apparent to the eye. She is simply an illustration of the argument I have been advancing—that our worst enemy is ignorance. Ignorance—you understand me? Since I have got you here, sir, I am going to hold you until I have managed to cure a little of your ignorance! For I tell you, sir, it is a thing which drives me to distraction—we MUST do something about these conditions! Take this case, for example. Here is a woman who is very seriously infected. I told her—well, wait; you shall see for yourself."

The doctor went to the door and summoned into the room a woman whom Monsieur Loches had noticed waiting there. She was verging on old age, small, frail, and ill-nourished in appearance, poorly dressed, and yet with a suggestion of refinement about her. She stood near the door, twisting her hands together nervously, and shrinking from the gaze of the strange gentleman. The doctor began in an angry voice. "Did I not tell you to come and see me once every eight days? Is that not true?"

The woman answered, in a faint voice, "Yes, sir."

"Well," he exclaimed, "and how long has it been since you were here?"

"Three months, sir."

"Three months! And you believe that I can take care of you under such conditions? I give you up! Do you understand? You discourage me, you discourage me." There was a pause. Then, seeing the woman's suffering, he began, in a gentler tone, "Come now, what is the reason that you have not come? Didn't you know that you have a serious disease—most serious?"

"Oh, yes, sir," replied the woman, "I know that very well—since my husband died of it."

The doctor's voice bore once again its note of pity. "Your husband died of it?"

"Yes, sir."

"He took no care of himself?"

"No, sir."

"And was not that a warning to you?"

"Doctor," the woman replied, "I would ask nothing better than to come as often as you told me, but the cost is too great."

"How—what cost? You were coming to my free clinic."

"Yes, sir," replied the woman, "but that's during working hours, and then it is a long way from home. There are so many sick people, and I have to wait my turn, It is in the morning—sometimes I lose a whole day—and then my employer is annoyed, and he threatens to turn me off. It is things like that that keep people from coming, until they dare not put it off any longer. Then, too, sir—" the woman stopped, hesitating.

"Well," demanded the doctor.

"Oh, nothing, sir," she stammered. "You have been too good to me already."

"Go on," commanded the other. "Tell me."

"Well," murmured the woman, "I know I ought not to put on airs, but you see I have not always been so poor. Before my husband's misfortune, we were well fixed. So you see, I have a little pride. I have always managed to take care of myself. I am not a woman of the streets, and to stand around like that, with everybody else, to be obliged to tell all one's miseries out loud before the world! I am wrong, I know it perfectly well; I argue with myself—but all the same, it's hard, sir; I assure you, it is truly hard."

"Poor woman!" said the doctor; and for a while there was a silence. Then he asked: "It was your husband who brought you the disease?"

"Yes, sir," was the reply. "Everything which happened to us came from him. We were living in the country when he got the disease. He went half crazy. He no longer knew how to manage his affairs. He gave orders here and there for considerable sums. We were not able to find the money."

"Why did he not undergo treatment?"

"He didn't know then. We were sold out, and we came to Paris. But we hadn't a penny. He decided to go to the hospital for treatment."

"And then?"

"Why, they looked him over, but they refused him any medicine."

"How was that?"

"Because we had been in Paris only three months. If one hasn't been a resident six months, one has no right to free medicine."

"Is that true?" broke in Monsieur Loches quickly.

"Yes," said the doctor, "that's the rule."

"So you see," said the woman, "it was not our fault."

"You never had children?" inquired the doctor.

"I was never able to bring one to birth," was the answer. "My husband was taken just at the beginning of our marriage—it was while he was serving in the army. You know, sir—there are women about the garrisons—" She stopped, and there was a long silence.

"Come," said the doctor, "that's all right. I will arrange it with you. You can come here to my office, and you can come on Sunday mornings." And as the poor creature started to express her gratitude, he slipped a coin into her hand. "Come, come; take it," he said gruffly. "You are not going to play proud with me. No, no, I have no time to listen to you. Hush!" And he pushed her out of the door.

Then he turned to the deputy. "You heard her story, sir," he said. "Her husband was serving his time in the army; it was you law-makers who compelled him to do that. And there are women about the garrisons—you heard how her voice trembled as she said that? Take my advice, sir, and look up the statistics as to the prevalence of this disease among our soldiers. Come to some of my clinics, and let me introduce you to other social types. You don't care very much about soldiers, perhaps—they belong to the lower classes, and you think of them as rough men. But let me show you what is going on among our college students—among the men our daughters are some day to marry. Let me show you the women who prey upon them! Perhaps, who knows—I can show you the very woman who was the cause of all the misery in your own family!"

And as Monsieur Loches rose from his chair, the doctor came to him and took him by the hand. "Promise me, sir," he said, earnestly, "that you will come back and let me teach you more about these matters. It is a chance that I must not let go—the first time in my life that I ever got hold of a real live deputy! Come and make a study of this subject, and let us try to work out some sensible plan, and get seriously to work to remedy these frightful evils!"

CHAPTER VI

George lived with his mother after Henriette had left his home. He was wretchedly unhappy and lonely. He could find no interest in any of the things which had pleased him before. He was ashamed to meet any of his friends, because he imagined that everyone must have heard the dreadful story—or because he was not equal to making up explanations for his mournful state. He no longer cared much about his work. What was the use of making a reputation or earning large fees when one had nothing to spend them for?

All his thoughts were fixed upon the wife and child he had lost. He was reminded of Henriette in a thousand ways, and each way brought him a separate pang of grief. He had never realized how much he had come to depend upon her in every little thing—until now, when her companionship was withdrawn from him, and everything seemed to be a blank. He would come home at night, and opposite to him at the dinner-table would be his mother, silent and spectral. How different from the days when Henriette was there, radiant and merry, eager to be told everything that had happened to him through the day!

There was also his worry about little Gervaise. He might no longer hear how she was doing, for he could not get up courage to ask his mother the news. Thus poor George was paying for his sins. He could make no complaints against the price, however high—only sometimes he wondered whether he would be able to pay it. There were times of such discouragement that he thought of different ways of killing himself.

A curious adventure befell him during this period. He was walking one day in the park, when he saw approaching a girl whose face struck him as familiar. At first he could not recollect where he had seen her. It was only when she was nearly opposite him that he realized—it was the girl who had been the cause of all his misery!

He tried to look away, but he was too late. Her eyes had caught his, and she nodded and then stopped, exclaiming, "Why, how do you do?"

George had to face her. "How do you do?" he responded, weakly.

She held out her hand and he had to take it, but there was not much welcome in his clasp. "Where have you been keeping yourself?" she asked. Then, as he hesitated, she laughed good-naturedly, "What's the matter? You don't seem glad to see me."

The girl—Therese was her name—had a little package under her arm, as if she had been shopping. She was not well dressed, as when George had met her before, and doubtless she thought that was the reason for his lack of cordiality. This made him rather ashamed, and so, only half realizing what he was doing, he began to stroll along with her.

"Why did you never come to see me again?" she asked.

George hesitated. "I—I—" he stammered—"I've been married since then."

She laughed. "Oh! So that's it!" And then, as they came to a bench under some trees, "Won't you sit down a while?" There was allurement in her glance, but it made George shudder. It was incredible to him that he had ever been attracted by this crude girl. The spell was now broken completely.

She quickly saw that something was wrong. "You don't seem very cheerful," she said. "What's the matter?"

And the man, staring at her, suddenly blurted out, "Don't you know what you did to me?"

"What I did to you?" Therese repeated wonderingly.

"You must know!" he insisted.

And then she tried to meet his gaze and could not. "Why—" she stammered.

There was silence between them. When George spoke again his voice was low and trembling. "You ruined my whole life," he said—"not only mine, but my family's. How could you do it?"

She strove to laugh it off. "A cheerful topic for an afternoon stroll!"

For a long while George did not answer. Then, almost in a whisper, he repeated, "How could you do it?"

"Some one did it to me first," was the response. "A man!"

"Yes," said George, "but he didn't know."

"How can you tell whether he knew or not?"

"You knew?" he inquired, wonderingly.

Therese hesitated. "Yes, I knew," she said at last, defiantly. "I have known for years."

"And I'm not the only man."

She laughed. "I guess not!"

There followed a long pause. At last he resumed, "I don't want to blame you; there's nothing to be gained by that; it's done, and can't be undone. But sometimes I wonder about it. I should like to understand—why did you do it?"

"Why? That's easy enough. I did it because I have to live."

"You live that way?" he exclaimed.

"Why of course. What did you think?"

"I thought you were a—a—" He hesitated.

"You thought I was respectable," laughed Therese. "Well, that's just a little game I was playing on you."

"But I didn't give you any money!" he argued.

"Not that time," she said, "but I thought you would come back."

He sat gazing at her. "And you earn your living that way still?" he asked. "When you know what's the matter with you! When you know—"

"What can I do? I have to live, don't I?"

"But don't you even take care of yourself? Surely there must be some way, some place—"

"The reformatory, perhaps," she sneered. "No, thanks! I'll go there when the police catch me, not before. I know some girls that have tried that."

"But aren't you afraid?" cried the man. "And the things that will happen to you! Have you ever talked to a doctor—or read a book?"

"I know," she said. "I've seen it all. If it comes to me, I'll go over the side of one of the bridges some dark night."

George sat lost in thought. A strange adventure it seemed to him— to meet this girl under such different circumstances! It was as if he were watching a play from behind the scenes instead of in front. If only he had had this new view in time—how different would have been his life! And how terrible it was to think of the others who didn't know—the audience who were still sitting out in front, watching the spectacle, interested in it!

His thoughts came back to Therese. He was curious about her and the life she lived. "Tell me a little about it," he said. "How you came to be doing this." And he added, "Don't think I want to preach; I'd really like to understand."

"Oh, it's a common story," she said—"nothing especially romantic.

I came to Paris when I was a girl. My parents had died, and I had no friends, and I didn't know what to do. I got a place as a nursemaid. I was seventeen years old then, and I didn't know anything. I believed what I was told, and I believed my employer. His wife was ill in a hospital, and he said he wanted to marry me when she died. Well, I liked him, and I was sorry for him—and then the first thing I knew I had a baby. And then the wife came back, and I was turned off. I had been a fool, of course. If I had been in her place should have done just what she did."

The girl was speaking in a cold, matter-of-fact voice, as of things about which she was no longer able to suffer. "So, there I was—on the street," she went on. "You have always had money, a comfortable home, education, friends to help you—all that. You can't imagine how it is to be in the world without any of these things. I lived on my savings as long as I could; then I had to leave my baby in a foundling's home, and I went out to do my five hours on the boulevards. You know the game, I have no doubt."

Yes, George knew the game. Somehow or other he no longer felt bitter towards this poor creature. She was part of the system of which he was a victim also. There was nothing to be gained by hating each other. Just as the doctor said, what was needed was enlightenment. "Listen," he said, "why don't you try to get cured?"

"I haven't got the price," was the answer.

"Well," he said, hesitatingly, "I know a doctor—one of the really good men. He has a free clinic, and I've no doubt he would take you in if I asked him to."

"YOU ask him?" echoed the other, looking at George in surprise.

The young man felt somewhat uncomfortable. He was not used to playing the role of the good Samaritan. "I—I need not tell him about us," he stammered. "I could just say that I met you. I have had such a wretched time myself, I feel sorry for anybody that's in the same plight. I should like to help you if I could."

The girl sat staring before her, lost in thought. "I have treated you badly, I guess," she said. "I'm sorry. I'm ashamed of myself."

George took a pencil and paper from his pocket and wrote the doctor's address. "Here it is," he said, in a business-like way, because he felt that otherwise he could become sentimental. He was half tempted to tell the woman what had happened to him, and all about Henriette and the sick child; but he realized that that would not do. So he rose and shook hands with her and left.

The next time he saw the doctor he told him about this girl. He decided to tell him the truth—having already made so many mistakes trying to conceal things. The doctor agreed to treat the woman, making the condition that George promise not to see her again.

The young man was rather shocked at this. "Doctor," he exclaimed, "I assure you you are mistaken. The thing you have in mind would be utterly impossible."

"I know," said the other, "you think so. But I think, young man, that I know more about life than you do. When a man and a woman have once committed such a sin, it is easy for them to slip back. The less time they spend talking about their misfortunes, and being generous and forbearing to each other, the better for them both."

"But, Doctor," cried George. "I love Henriette! I could not possibly love anyone else. It would be horrible to me!"

"Yes," said the doctor. "But you are not living with Henriette. You are wandering round, not knowing what to do with yourself next."

There was no need for anybody to tell George that. "What do you think?" he asked abruptly. "Is there any hope for me?"

"I think there is," said the other, who, in spite of his resolution, had become a sort of ambassador for the unhappy husband. He had to go to the Loches house to attend the child, and so he could not help seeing Henriette, and talking to her about the child's health and her own future. He considered that George had had his lesson, and urged upon the young wife that he would be wiser in future, and safe to trust.

George had indeed learned much. He got new lessons every time he went to call at the physician's office—he could read them in the faces of the people he saw there. One day when he was alone in the waiting-room, the doctor came out of his inner office, talking to an elderly gentleman, whom George recognized as the father of one of his classmates at college. The father was a little shopkeeper, and the young man remembered how pathetically proud he had been of his son. Could it be, thought George, that this old man was a victim of syphilis?

But it was the son, and not the father, who was the subject of the consultation. The old man was speaking in a deeply moved voice, and he stood so that George could not help hearing what he said. "Perhaps you can't understand," he said, "just what it means to us—the hopes we had of that boy! Such a fine fellow he was, and a good fellow, too, sir! We were so proud of him; we had bled our veins to keep him in college—and now just see!"

"Don't despair, sir," said the doctor, "we'll try to cure him." And he added with that same note of sorrow in his voice which George had heard, "Why did you wait so long before you brought the boy to me?"

"How was I to know what he had?" cried the other. "He didn't dare tell me, sir—he was afraid of my scolding him. And in the meantime the disease was running its course. When he realized that he had it, he went secretly to one of the quacks, who robbed him, and didn't cure him. You know how it is, sir."

"Yes, I know," said the doctor.

"Such things ought not to be permitted," cried the old man. "What is our government about that it allows such things to go on? Take the conditions there at the college where my poor boy was ruined.

At the very gates of the building these women are waiting for the lads! Ought they to be permitted to debauch young boys only fifteen years old? Haven't we got police enough to prevent a thing like that? Tell me, sir!"

"One would think so," said the doctor, patiently.

"But is it that the police don't want to?"

"No doubt they have the same excuse as all the rest—they don't know. Take courage, sir; we have cured worse cases than your son's. And some day, perhaps, we shall be able to change these conditions."

So he went on with the man, leaving George with something to think about. How much he could have told them about what had happened to that young fellow when only fifteen years old! It had not been altogether the fault of the women who were lurking outside of the college gates; it was a fact that the boy's classmates had teased him and ridiculed him, had literally made his life a torment, until he had yielded to temptation.

It was the old, old story of ignorant and unguided schoolboys all over the world! They thought that to be chaste was to be weak and foolish; that a fellow was not a man unless he led a life of debauchery like the rest. And what did they know about these dreadful diseases? They had the most horrible superstitions—ideas of cures so loathsome that they could not be set down in print; ideas as ignorant and destructive as those of savages in the heart of Africa. And you might hear them laughing and jesting about one another's condition. They might be afflicted with diseases which would have the most terrible after-effects upon their whole lives and upon their families—diseases which cause tens of thousands of surgical operations upon women, and a large percentage of blindness and idiocy in children—and you might hear them confidently express the opinion that these diseases were no worse than a bad cold!

And all this mass of misery and ignorance covered over and clamped down by a taboo of silence, imposed by the horrible superstition of sex-prudery! George went out from the doctor's office trembling with excitement over this situation. Oh, why had not some one warned him in time? Why didn't the doctors and the teachers lift up their voices and tell young men about these frightful dangers? He wanted to go out in the highways and preach it himself—except that he dared not, because he could not explain to the world his own sudden interest in this forbidden topic.

These was only one person he dared to talk to: that was his mother—to whom he ought to have talked many, many years before. He was moved to mention to her the interview he had overheard in the doctor's office. In a sudden burst of grief he told her of his struggles and temptations; he pleaded with her to go to Henriette once more—to tell her these things, and try to make her realize that he alone was not to blame for them, that they were a condition which prevailed everywhere, that the only difference between her husband and other men was that he had had the misfortune to be caught.

There was pressure being applied to Henriette from several sides. After all, what could she do? She was comfortable in her father's home, so far as the physical side of things went; but she knew that all her friends were gossiping and speculating about her separation from her husband, and sooner or later she would have to make up her mind, either to separate permanently from George or to return to him. There was not much happiness for her in the thought of getting a divorce from a man whom deep in her heart she loved. She would be practically a widow the rest of her life, and the home in which poor little Gervaise would be brought up would not be a cheerful one.

George was ready to offer any terms, if only she would come back to his home. They might live separate lives for as long as Henriette wished. They would have no more children until the doctor declared it was quite safe; and in the meantime he would be humble and patient, and would try his best to atone for the wrong that he had done her.

To these arguments Madame Dupont added others of her own. She told the girl some things which through bitter experience she had learned about the nature and habits of men; things that should be told to every girl before marriage, but which almost all of them are left to find out afterwards, with terrible suffering and disillusionment. Whatever George's sins may have been, he was a man who had been chastened by suffering, and would know how to value a woman's love for the rest of his life. Not all men knew that—not even those who had been fortunate in escaping from the so-called "shameful disease."

Henriette was also hearing arguments from her father, who by this time had had time to think things over, and had come to the conclusion that the doctor was right. He had noted his son-in-law's patience and penitence, and had also made sure that in spite of everything Henriette still loved him. The baby apparently was doing well; and the Frenchman, with his strong sense of family ties, felt it a serious matter to separate a child permanently from its father. So in the end he cast the weight of his influence in favor of a reconciliation, and Henriette returned to her husband, upon terms which the doctor laid down.

The doctor played in these negotiations the part which he had not been allowed to play in the marriage. For the deputy was now thoroughly awake to the importance of the duty he owed his daughter. In fact, he had become somewhat of a "crank" upon the whole subject. He had attended several of the doctor's clinics, and had read books and pamphlets on the subject of syphilis, and was now determined that there should be some practical steps towards reform.

At the outset, he had taken the attitude of the average legislator, that the thing to do was to strengthen the laws against prostitution, and to enforce them more strictly. He echoed the cry of the old man whom George had heard in the doctor's office: "Are there not enough police?"

"We must go to the source," he declared. "We must proceed against these miserable women—veritable poisoners that they are!"

He really thought this was going to the source! But the doctor was quick to answer his arguments. "Poisoners?" he said. "You forget that they have first been poisoned. Every one of these women who communicates the disease has first received it from some man."

Monsieur Loches advanced to his second idea, to punish the men. But the doctor had little interest in this idea either. He had seen it tried so many times—such a law could never be enforced. What must come first was education, and by this means a modification of morals. People must cease to treat syphilis as a mysterious evil, of which not even the name could be pronounced.

"But," objected the other, "one cannot lay it bare to children in our educational institutions!"

"Why not?" asked the doctor.

"Because, sir, there are curiosities which it would be imprudent to awaken."

The doctor became much excited whenever he heard this argument. "You believe that you are preventing these curiosities from awakening?" he demanded. "I appeal to those—both men and women—who have passed through colleges and boarding schools! Such curiosities cannot be smothered, and they satisfy themselves as best they can, basely, vilely. I tell you, sir, there is nothing immoral about the act which perpetuates life by means of love. But we organize around it, so far as concerns our children, a gigantic and rigorous conspiracy of silence. The worthy citizen takes his daughter and his son to popular musical comedies, where they listen to things which would make a monkey blush; but it is forbidden to discuss seriously before the young that act of love which people seem to think they should only know of through blasphemies and profanations! Either that act is a thing of which people can speak without blushing—or else, sir, it is a matter for the innuendoes of the cabaret and the witticisms of the messroom! Pornography is admitted, but science is not! I tell you, sir, that is the thing which must be changed! We must elevate the soul of the young man by taking these facts out of the realm of mystery and of slang. We must awaken in him a pride in that creative power with which each one of us is endowed. We must make him understand that he is a sort of temple in which is prepared the future of the race, and we must teach him that he must transmit, intact, the heritage entrusted to him—the precious heritage which has been built out of the tears and miseries and sufferings of an interminable line of ancestors!"

So the doctor argued. He brought forth case after case to prove that the prostitute was what she was, not because of innate vileness, but because of economic conditions. It happened that the deputy came to one of the clinics where he met Therese. The doctor brought her into his consulting room, after telling her that the imposing-looking gentleman was a friend of the director of the opera, and might be able to recommend her for a position on the stage to which she aspired. "Tell him all about yourself," he said, "how you live, and what you do, and what you would like to do. You will get him interested in you."

So the poor girl retold the story of her life. She spoke in a matter-of-fact voice, and when she came to tell how she had been obliged to leave her baby in the foundling asylum, she was surprised that Monsieur Loches showed horror. "What could I do?" she demanded. "How could I have taken care of it?"

"Didn't you ever miss it?" he asked.

"Of course I missed it. But what difference did that make? It would have died of hunger with me."

"Still," he said, "it was your child—"

"It was the father's child, too, wasn't it? Much attention he paid to it! If I had been sure of getting money enough, I would have put it out to nurse. But with the twenty-five or thirty francs a month I could have earned as a servant, could I have paid for a baby? That's the situation a girl faces—so long as I wanted to remain honest, it was impossible for me to keep my child. You answer, perhaps, 'You didn't stay honest anyway.' That's true. But then—when you are hungry, and a nice young fellow offers you dinner, you'd have to be made of wood to refuse him. Of course, if I had had a trade—but I didn't have any. So I went on the street—You know how it is."

"Tell us about it," said the doctor. "This gentleman is from the country."

"Is that so?" said the girl. "I never supposed there was anyone who didn't know about such things. Well, I took the part of a little working-girl. A very simple dress—things I had made especially for that—a little bundle in a black napkin carried in my hand—so I walked along where the shops are. It's tiresome, because to do it right, you have to patter along fast. Then I stop before a shop, and nine times out of ten, there you are! A funny thing is that the men—you'd imagine they had agreed on the words to approach you with. They have only two phrases; they never vary them. It's either, 'You are going fast, little one.' Or it's, 'Aren't you afraid all alone?' One thing or the other. One knows pretty well what they mean. Isn't it so?" The girl paused, then went on. "Again, I would get myself up as a young widow. There, too, one has to walk fast: I don't know why that should be so, but it is. After a minute or two of conversation, they generally find out that I am not a young widow, but that doesn't make any difference—they go on just the same."

"Who are the men?" asked the deputy. "Clerks? Traveling salesmen?"

"Not much," she responded. "I keep a lookout for gentlemen—like yourself."

"They SAY they are gentlemen," he suggested.

"Sometimes I can see it," was the response. "Sometimes they wear orders. It's funny—if they have on a ribbon when you first notice them, they follow you, and presto—the ribbon is gone! I always laugh over that. I've watched them in the glass of the shop windows. They try to look unconcerned, but as they walk along they snap out the ribbon with their thumb—as one shells little peas, you know."

She paused; then, as no one joined in her laugh, she continued, "Well, at last the police got after me, That's a story that I've never been able to understand. Those filthy men gave me a nasty disease, and then I was to be shut in prison for it! That was a little too much, it seems to me."

"Well," said the doctor, grimly, "you revenged yourself on them—from what you have told me."

The other laughed. "Oh, yes," she said. "I had my innings." She turned to Monsieur Loches. "You want me to tell you that? Well, just on the very day I learned that the police were after me, I was coming home furious, naturally. It was on the Boulevard St. Denis, if you know the place—and whom do you think I met? My old master—the one who got me into trouble, you know. There it was, God's own will! I said to myself, 'Now, my good fellow, here's the time where you pay me what you owe me, and with interest, too!' I put on a little smile—oh, it didn't take very long, you may be sure!"

The woman paused; her face darkened, and she went on, in a voice trembling with agitation: "When I had left him, I was seized with a rage. A sort of madness got into my blood. I took on all the men who offered themselves, for whatever they offered me, for nothing, if they didn't offer me anything. I took as many as I could, the youngest ones and the handsomest ones. Just so! I only gave them back what they had given to me. And since that time I haven't really cared about anyone any more. I just turned it all into a joke." She paused, and then looking at the deputy, and reading in his face the horror with which he was regarding her, "Oh, I am not the only one!" she exclaimed. "There are lots of other women who do the same. To be sure, it is not for vengeance—it is because they must have something to eat. For even if you have syphilis, you have to eat, don't you? Eh?"

She had turned to the doctor, but he did not answer. There was a long silence; and then thinking that his friend, the deputy, had heard enough for one session, the doctor rose. He dismissed the woman, the cause of all George Dupont's misfortunes, and turning to Monsieur Loches, said: "It was on purpose that I brought that wretched prostitute before you. In her the whole story is summed up—not merely the story of your son-in-law, but that of all the victims of the red plague. That woman herself is a victim, and she is a symbol of the evil which we have created and which falls upon our own heads again. I could add nothing to her story, I only ask you, Monsieur Loches—when next you are proposing new laws in the Chamber of Deputies, not to forget the horrors which that poor woman has exposed to you!"